RESTORATION

'More tales from the house that sat down'

Copyright

First Edition August 2017

ISBN 1548679100
ISBN 9781548679101

Cover design by Amanda Ní Odhráin
http://www.gobookyourself.info/p/design-services.html

The original oil painting 'Bluebells' used in the cover design is the work of Genevieve Alice May Tomkins (née Walshaw) © August 2017.

For
Gill and Nigel, Granma and Papa, Mum and Dad,
so many names for two very special people!

Also for Guinevere,
who is 'the little girl on a swing'.

Other books by Alice May:

Accidental Damage - tales from the house that sat down

Acknowledgements

There are so many people without whom this story would not have seen the light of day and I would like to take the opportunity to thank some of them here, so please bear with me.

Firstly I would like to thank all our family, friends, and neighbours who have been so kind and supportive during the true events that inspired this book. Also, thank you to the Barbarians' Godfather Neal, for turning up out of the blue one day armed with a day off work, overalls, rollers, trays, paint brushes and endless energy. You have no idea how much that meant to us Neal!

Similarly the whole family are very grateful to the fantastic staff members at the Barbarians' schools for all the support that was given to our children throughout the events that inspired both 'Accidental Damage' and 'Restoration'.

I would also like to thank the Dorset Taekwondo Association for making the whole family so welcome at training sessions. Who knew Taekwondo would be so much fun?
http://dtkd.co.uk/

I have met so many fantastic people on this 'author journey' of mine, not least of which is Gill Donnell (MBE) of the Successful Women Development Network, who makes such a point of encouraging women to reach their full potential. Gill you are inspirational!
https://www.facebook.com/SuccessfulWomen.training

By the same token, I must also thank Sharon White, a very talented mixed media artist, who has inspired and encouraged me not only in the creation of my artwork and associated products but also in telling my story.

Finally I'd like to thank my local Women's Institute for making me so very welcome.

CONTENTS

PART 1

Pre-amble

1: Re-evaluate
2: Transmute
3: Genesis
4: Juggernaut
5: Alchemy

PART 2

6: Synthesis
7: Infusion
8: Amalgamation
9: Tincture:
10: Re-energise

PART 3

11: Deconstruction
12: Practice
13: Quandary
14: Indomitable Spirit

PART 4

15: Integrity
16: Jamboree
17: Ramification
18: Perseverance

PART 5

19: Resurgence
20: Transfiguration
21: Evolution
22: Purgatory
23: Headway

PART 6

24: Exacting
25: Emergent
26: Culmination
27: Perseverance
28: Realisation
29: Apotheosis
Epilogue

PART 1

The (wo)man who moves a mountain begins by carrying away small stones

Confucius

Pre-amble – A word from the author to set the scene...

If you had told our heroine at 7am this morning that she would be on her knees, cradling a human head in the centre of the local town's high street by 9.09am, she wouldn't have believed you. She had no idea that it was going to be *one of those days*!

Welcome back my dear friends. It has been some time since last we spoke. I had intended to leave my story where it ended in Accidental Damage, but so many people have asked me 'What happened next?' that I have taken to my trusty, old keyboard again.

As you know we last saw our heroine in the arms of her beloved husband when he finally persuaded her to stop blaming herself for her part in the disaster that had befallen their home and had nearly torn their family apart. One might be forgiven for thinking that this was the end of the story, but it would seem not. There are some unforeseen consequences to those previous events, which are starting to make their presence felt and our heroine has her work cut out in order to sort them out.

We are soon to re-join her in both the present, approximately six months after we left her in Accidental Damage, and also in the past as the family struggle with the practicalities of rebuilding their home.

Let us begin with the present day because, as you can see from the above introductory statement, she is back in the thick of drama once again. Had she had any inkling of what fate had in store for her on that particular morning she would (quite understandably) have gone back to bed to wait for tomorrow. As it was, that morning started much like any other, as she sleepily listened to the radio whilst scraping three day old, concreted-on, Weetabix from a cereal bowl excavated from beneath her teenage son's bed.

'Cradling a human head?' you say. 'Why on earth is she doing that?'

Well I am glad you asked because I can assure you that she is not doing it for fun.

I'll let her tell you all about it now....

1: Re-evaluate

Definition: to consider something for a second time in order to judge value, quality or importance.

Present day...

It was quite unbelievable just how much my knees were hurting.

I tried unobtrusively to shift the weight on them without disturbing the head that I had clutched in my sweaty hands. The head is encased in a motorcycle helmet, a nice, black, shiny one. No doubt shiny, black helmets are very cool but they are also rather slippery. Don't panic though, the head was fully attached to the motorcyclist's body and that body did appear to still be breathing. (I don't do gratuitous gore and there's no need in this instance anyway, as the feared injuries turned out to be relatively minor in the end, but nobody knew that just then.)

I must confess that the reason I was coping with the scenario so well was the fact that I had my suspicions that the aforementioned motorcyclist was not particularly badly hurt, although I was certainly not going to say so out loud, as I could have been wrong. It has been known to happen.

Nevertheless, I had been afforded a ringside view of the motorbike rider overtaking the car in front of me as I sat stationary in my little, purple car at the traffic lights. The handlebars of the bike had unfortunately clipped the car wing mirror as it passed, setting the rider off on a somewhat wobbly and erratic course. All valiant attempts to bring the bike back under control ended in it rising up onto the back wheel to perform a slow and lazy pirouette, while dumping the rider on the ground before the machine bounded through a gap in the on-coming traffic and collided with a parked car on the other side of the road.

Ooops!

We all make mistakes, but this one was a spectacularly messy one, leaving bits of motorbike scattered everywhere, so I had immense sympathy with the rider on the ground before me. He had single-handedly caused all movement to come to an abrupt standstill on this busy high street at a critical point in the Monday morning rush hour. This was the only route through our busy market town, and as both sides of the road were now completely compromised, absolutely no one here would be getting to work or school on time.

If I were in his leathers, I think I would lie still and keep very quiet too.

I could hear multiple sirens heading our way indicating that the confident sounding gentleman, who had rushed out of the flower shop on hearing the sound of a collision and insisted on me holding the rider's head still, had successfully alerted the authorities. Excellent news!

Fortunately, just as I was thinking that I wasn't sure quite how much more my knees could take, I was distracted by the arrival of two enormously handsome paramedics. It's an ill wind that blows no one any good. I smiled up at them when they cheerfully introduced themselves before realising they were talking to the head in my hands and not the old woman holding it. I relinquished my hold on the helmet when asked to do so, brushed the ingrained grit and tarmac out of my kneecaps, and sat back to appreciate the much improved scenery, listening to the paramedics at work. They had opened the visor of the helmet (It hadn't occurred to me to do that, although in my defence I don't have three hands.) and were speaking gently to the casualty.

I was surprised to note two things. The rider was a very pretty, very young *she*, not a *he* at all. That'll teach me to make assumptions! I also noted, with some fascination, that she was in possession of very trendy black eyebrows (the sort that look like they've been drawn on using a marker pen) and the most abundant forest of fake eyelash extensions, complete with gemstone embellishments. It was quite impressive that she had managed to open her eyes at all under the sheer weight of these adornments, but fortunately she was managing to flutter them at the paramedics quite successfully, which suggested to me that she was probably OK. Relieved to see this, I excused myself and went to find a policeman to give my name and address to in case they needed a statement.

Give them their due, when they swing into action the British Traffic Police are very good at keeping things moving and it wasn't that long before we were all on our way again as soon as the lady with the eyelashes had been carted off in an ambulance.

I pulled away from the high street leaving the hustle and bustle of the town behind me, to head along empty country lanes in the direction of home. My plan for the morning had been to go to a local gallery and ask if they had any exhibition space but the drama of the last hour had rather put me off that idea. It was no great loss, I wasn't really sure I wanted to get back into exhibiting anyway. I just wanted to get on with the next painting, not faff around selling the last one. However, my Beloved Husband obviously feels entirely differently about the matter and had been making some very pointed comments recently suggesting that we might end up buried under finished canvases if we're (he means 'I'm') not careful. I don't know what he's on about. They are all carefully stored away in my little studio.

Ok and the shed (it's a small one).......and part of the garage (not a small one). I suppose there are a few behind the sofa, and there's a really big one stuffed down the side of the freezer too. Hmm! Maybe he has a point. I will have to get it sorted out, but not today.

Twenty minutes later I pulled onto the drive back at the cottage and was rather shocked to see a 'For Sale' sign emerging from our front hedge. Wow! That hadn't been there when I left, although I shouldn't really be surprised, as we had discussed putting the house on the market. Nevertheless I wasn't quite prepared for the reality of it. I guess it's a bit like the difference between the suspicion that the mobile speed camera probably caught you and the actual police enforcement notice landing on your doormat.

It would seem that we were now the proud clients of an extremely enthusiastic and efficient estate agent. This was a very new development but one which Beloved Husband and I had always suspected might be the final price to pay for the events of three years ago. You might say that the writing had been on the crumbly cottage walls all along in spite of everything we had done to try to prevent it.

Now, I don't know about you, but I hate it when I am reading a sequel and the author spends at least two chapters bringing me up to date with what happened in the first book. It's a waste of time, paper and ink in my opinion, so if you haven't read Accidental Damage, I would politely suggest that you probably should before continuing with this book.

Having said that though, there is something I didn't mention previously, about those early days after the cottage started to crumble, that you do need to know for the continuation of my tale, and so I'll explain that here. I'll be quick, I promise!

You already know that a large part of our three hundred and fifty year old cob cottage started to disintegrate one day leaving the vast majority of our home uninhabitable and forcing us to move into a tent in the garden while we tried to work out what to do about it.

You also know that we spent quite some time trying to salvage our possessions from the wibbly, wobbly part of the house and that we continued to use a ground floor kitchen/lounge/conservatory extension built at the back of the property even though we didn't know if it was entirely stable.

What you don't know is that there was one small bedroom that was built over part of that extension. Now going on the theory that the kitchen/lounge/conservatory might be stable and therefore safe to use, there was a chance that this bedroom was too. Both had been built more recently than the cob section of the house and we hoped the old bit falling wouldn't pull the newer part down as well. Unfortunately we were unable to access this bedroom as to get there you had to go through the crumbling cob section and climb the collapsing staircase. Not really advisable under the circumstances.

In a moment of madness back then, we had considered cutting a hole up into this room from the kitchen ceiling below and using a ladder to reach it at night, we were so desperate for more civilised sleeping accommodation than the tent. Fortunately, reason returned before we did this, as smashing holes in the bit of the house that was still standing, was never going to be a terribly inspired idea at the best of times, but let's face it we weren't really thinking clearly back then.

You will no doubt remember that, in the initial aftermath of the cob collapse, we had systematically (and some would say foolishly) stripped the damaged section of the house of all our belongings using a slowly disintegrating staircase that behaved rather like the enchanted staircases at Hogwarts. The treads moved underfoot and the whole stairwell seemed determined to reconfigure itself as we passed, with chunks of masonry falling at random just to spice things up a bit.

Accepting that it wouldn't be long before someone was injured or killed on route, we made one final trip upstairs, during which my Beloved Husband and I hauled anything left (apart from a really heavy wardrobe in our son Quiet's room that we had to abandon where it was) through into that little, back bedroom and stacked it up as neatly as possible. These were items that we hoped we would be able to manage without for an indefinable period of time, as once the door was sealed off (using insulating board and thick layers of industrial tape to keep the worst of the weather and the dust out) there would be no way back in until the house had been repaired.

One such abandoned item sat in the sunshine on the windowsill of that sealed room. A half completed oil painting of a little girl on a swing, my creation of which had been rudely interrupted by the collapse of the house. Over the next year the little girl would stand guard in suspended animation over the entombed contents of that room, the partially completed oily brush strokes of her face hardening off and drying in the sunshine, a colourful testimony to the suddenness with which our contented, ordinary life had ceased that day.

***

Sat in my car on the drive staring at the brand new Estate Agent board, I could remember quite clearly sealing up that little back bedroom and recalled how, at that moment, I hadn't been entirely sure that a time would ever come when I would be able to enter it again. There were a lot of hard decisions and plenty of tears to get through before such an event could come about, with no guarantee of success.

I sighed heavily. It was no good! The collision earlier that morning had certainly unsettled me but the arrival of this For Sale sign, such visual evidence of our failure to save the house, compounded things. I was going to have to paint while I sorted things out in my head. Opening the car door and stepping out I noticed a small white feather lying on the ground at my feet. Absent-mindedly I reached down to pick it up, but as I rose I noticed a sudden light headed feeling and an odd fluttery sensation in my chest. 'Silly woman,' I thought to myself, ‘you stood up too quickly. Pull yourself together!’

Taking a couple of deep breaths and shaking my head to clear it I slammed the car door and headed into the empty house, my footsteps echoing in the hallway as I marched directly to my little art studio next to the stairs. Putting the feather on the window sill in the sunshine where the cat used to sleep, I turned on the radio and started pulling out brushes and tubes of paint.

2: Transmute

Definition: to change something from one form to another, or to be changed in this way

Staying in the present....

It wasn't long before I was settled in front of my easel with a canvas primed and loaded brush poised. I could already feel myself beginning to relax a bit.

You might ask why I found myself in such a contemplative mood. It's only a For Sale sign after all! It's not quite that simple though; things never are, are they? We had fought so hard to keep our Barbarians together when the house fell down and we had succeeded against the odds. But things change and now the oldest ones are starting to leave us of their own accord. Even though I don't like it, I do have to accept it. After all, that is life! It is time for them to move forwards, and it's not fair to make them do it whilst dragging their mother kicking and screaming behind them.

Don't get me wrong, I was pleased that our two girls, Chaos and Logic, were going to university, but simultaneously I missed them. How dare they leave me, but didn't they do well? A contrary little yin and yang to keep me endlessly entertained!

It needs to be appreciated that the absence of two girls changes the balance in a home significantly. I found myself abandoned in a very a male dominated environment consisting of Beloved Husband and our two boy Barbarians, (significantly-less) Quiet and (not-quite-so) Small.

Now that Chaos and Logic were not around talking all the time Quiet seemed to have found his voice, albeit a voice that operated in an entirely different register than it had before. (When did that happen?) He was now in sole charge of a dangerously deep vocal instrument and took great delight in creeping up behind me and making sudden loud sounds that reverberated in a booming bass register, for no other apparent reason than to see me jump out of my skin before he ambled off grinning contentedly to himself. (Bless!!)

Whereas Small just kept on growing! No doubt this had something to do with the colossal amount of food he managed to eat every single day. I had noticed recently though that, at the same time as continuously consuming calories, he seemed to need to incessantly ingest information. He was always asking questions. Intelligent ones! Most of which I didn't know the answers to. Sometimes I suspected that the little smart Alec realised that and was only asking so that he could watch me squirm. (For goodness' sake, he wasn't even out of primary school yet! Thank heaven for Google, is all I can say on that one!)

For so many years it seemed that our home was knee high with toddlers complete with the associated noise, exhaustion, mess, mayhem and fun that all that involved. Yet now all too soon the eldest two had grown and flown. It required serious adjustment, especially for a control freak like me! Even my cat had abandoned me in the most ultimate way possible and I found that I missed the disdainful looks she used to give me and her smug attitude way more than I had ever expected to.

Restoration

Don't get me wrong the house was still filled with commotion and noise, the boy Barbarians saw to that, but there was still something missing. It was hard to put a finger on it. In the blink of an eye, there were simply not enough people in this cottage anymore and I didn't like it one little bit.

Nevertheless, it is the natural order of things and I had to adjust. After all if they didn't leave home at all then I would be grumbling about that wouldn't I?

I know!

There's just no pleasing me.

***

A little while later on, when I had worked up quite a thirst throwing paint at the canvas, I started to run out of steam. Looking round for sustenance I realised that I was going to have to shift for myself if I wanted a cup of tea.

Ten minutes after that, having investigated all kitchen cupboards while the kettle boiled and failed to unearth anything remotely sugar based, I wandered out into the front garden to sit on my little wrought iron bench in the sunshine clutching a steaming mug of tea.

I couldn't help thinking of another time when I had sat here over three years previously, bundled up against the cold in almost every layer of clothing I possessed and clutching a cup of tea, while I nervously awaited the arrival of the promised builders to begin the rebuild process of our beautiful but wobbly cottage.

We had been assured that the building team would arrive at 9am on January 2nd, almost six months from the day that the walls had fallen. I remembered sitting in this exact same spot on that day waiting for them and how I couldn't quite believe that it would actually happen.

At that time, the front and side walls of the main (damaged) section of what was a three hundred and fifty year old cob cottage were encased in thick sheets of black plastic and were propped up with a random selection of scaffolding poles, wedges and strong-boys, some inside and some outside. These props were attempting to prevent any further slippage but I was pretty certain that incremental movement was still merrily underway. Amazingly, the beautiful, thatched roof appeared totally unaffected by the almost complete lack of support from two of the walls beneath it.

As I had sat there waiting for my promised builders, I had found myself wondering exactly what sort of state the house would be in, under all that plastic, having been abandoned for so long through the cold wet months of the autumn and early winter. The smell emanating from beneath the protective covering was a disturbing one of overpowering damp and rot.

The black sheeting effectively hid the extent of the damage to the casual observer, but beneath all the plastic were two huge cracks, one in each of two main supporting walls, that ran the full height of the building from the ground to the roof. One of the cracks, when I had last set eyes on it before the plastic encased it, was large enough for a fully-grown person to walk straight into the house (followed closely by a friendly dog of unknown origin). Windows hung at odd angles or had fallen out completely, old lathe and plaster internal walls were destroyed and ceilings had come down. Hidden in the all-encompassing darkness created by the plastic sheeting, over in the far right hand corner of the ground floor were the remaining treads of that magically morphing staircase I mentioned.

Admittedly, we took huge risks by continuing to use the potentially unstable single storey kitchen/lounge extension, with its little bathroom, right at the back of the house during the months of negotiations that took place with our house insurance company to decide who was liable for the cost of the repair.

All the while a very real game of Russian roulette was played on a daily basis. In fact, the whole home collapse scenario had successfully redefined what constituted sensible behaviour for all of us and we quickly became fairly blasé about spending time in what was effectively part of an old ruin that might come tumbling down around our ears at any moment. We grew to be quite comfortable living with one eye constantly on the nearest exit, ready to escape in seconds if needed. A habit which, I can assure you, never really leaves you once it is learned!

During all those months of living in a sort of suspended animation, not knowing if an agreement would ever be reached with our house insurance company that might enable us to move the situation forward, we became almost philosophical in our defiance of danger. My though processes often ran along the lines of 'I'm cold and I'm tired. The house is not actually falling down right at this particular minute and I want a hot shower. Therefore I'm going to have a hot shower. If I get squashed then I get squashed. So be it!'

But all that was about to change! An agreement had been reached. That cold, fresh January day was one of positivity. It was a massive turning point. There would be no more marking time, stagnating and waiting for progress to start. That day we would start to rebuild our home and move forward with our lives.

Assuming the builders ever turned up of course!

So let's stay with the past and see what actually happened.....

3: Genesis

Definition: beginning, origin or mode of creation of something.

Back in the past: Day 1 of the long awaited house repair job

In the beginning.......it was so very cold.

I had been waiting on the driveway since 8.40am alternately hopeful for a start to the rebuild and already despairing that the promised builders genuinely might not turn up. Nothing else in this whole fiasco had gone smoothly so far, so I felt I could be forgiven for being a bit mistrustful.

The Barbarians were all slumbering peacefully (I lie, they were all snoring loudly!) away in their various cosy nests in the caravan, but I had been up horribly early as usual. I had carefully applied multiple layers of clothing and then sneaked out of the caravan, trying not to wake the slumbering snoozers, before scuttling barefoot across the icy cold paving slabs to the patio, wishing I had remembered to take my slippers out to the caravan with me the night before.

Skirting around Skelly, (a fake – at least I hope so - skeleton which had arrived for the Barbarians' Halloween party last November and never really left) who was sitting in a deck chair next to our potted outdoor Christmas tree outside the conservatory, I noted absently that someone had thoughtfully supplied him with a hat, a blanket and *my* slippers!

So that's where they were! I bent down to retrieve my pilfered footwear then, before my frozen feet actually fell off, I hastened through the French doors into the back section of the house.

Once inside I shivered violently as I speedily stuffed ten icy toes into my slippers and waited impatiently for the kettle to boil, hopping painfully from one frozen appendage to the other in the hope that the action would restore circulation. This activity was interrupted by the cat reluctantly peeling herself away from the stone hearth and any dwindling residual heat from yesterday's fire to loudly demand sustenance.

Having dealt with the famished feline, I scouted around the accessible bit of the house for any other items of attire that I could put on, including a padded body warmer that was the perfect size to allow me to shove a mini heart-shaped hot water bottle just inside the front zipper at chest height. This had the double advantage of keeping me warm and made me look like I had had a significant bust augmentation.

Eventually I had to stop putting on clothes because, firstly, I ran out of them, and secondly, I was about to lose the ability to bend and/or breathe if I added any more. This getting dressed lark wasn't a random process by the way. I had had months to perfect the precise sequence of layers of clothes that enabled me to get the most on, promoted the maximum body-heat-retention whilst maintaining a basic efficiency of physical movement. I could write a detailed article on it for some science journal, if I had the time, assuming anyone was remotely interested of course. After all I do have a science degree, you know, I am not just the slightly mad, art-obsessed owner of a crumbly cottage in the country.

So anyway, half an hour later there I was, sat on my little wrought iron bench by the garage, with a cup of tea waiting nervously for someone to turn up.

Anyone!

Fortunately I didn't have to wait that long. I could hear the gunning of a straining engine long before a white van swung speedily onto our drive and ground to a halt churning up a bow wave of pea-shingle before it. 'An interesting start,' I thought to myself struggling to my feet.

The van door swung open forcibly and a man got out.

At first glance I could tell he was a very cross and grumpy man.

"Do you have any idea how long it's taken me to find you?" Grumpy Van Man shouted accusingly at me, without so much as an attempt at 'hello,' or even 'good morning.'

"Um! No?" I swallowed nervously taking a small step back, rather wishing he hadn't found me. This was not a promising development.

"What does anyone want to live way out here for? It's the middle of nowhere!" He continued.

I refrained from pointing out that usually, living way out here meant I didn't have to deal with people like him. Instead I bit my tongue. Hard! Some of us were brought up with good manners.

He opened the back door of his van and rummaged noisily around in it for a few moments. As I watched him nervously I was distracted by something brushing past my face very gently. Looking down quickly I saw a small white feather had landed on my augmented bust-line. Carefully picking it off, I examined it absently.

“So!” barked Grumpy. “Where are these solar panels you want installed then?”

What? I shoved the little feather into my pocket and looked at him startled. Then I registered what he’d actually said.

Thank goodness!

I don’t think many people smile at Grumpy (Which is not really surprising given his attitude.) because he looked most disconcerted when I beamed at him in response to his rude question. But the sheer relief that he obviously wasn’t my much awaited builders was almost impossible to hide.

“I am sorry but I think you are in the wrong place,” I said, whilst probably not looking remotely apologetic.

“I am not in the wrong place!” he replied forcefully, “my satnav says the solar farm is here.” He jabbed his right forefinger firmly toward the ground at his feet.

“It might well say that,” I agreed, looking from him to the wobbly walls of my house. “But can you actually see a solar farm here?”

"It must be here somewhere," he said belligerently, while looking suspiciously around him at the driveway and then at me as if he thought I was playing some kind of trick on him.

I ask you! Seriously! Where on earth would I hide a solar farm? And more importantly, why? I didn't have time for silly games with grumpy strangers. I just wanted some builders to fix my house, hopefully nice ones and preferably today.

"You are on the right road," I said encouragingly, "only you're a few miles out. It's that way!" I pointed helpfully along the lane.

He looked as if he wanted to argue with me but I wasn't planning on sticking around to listen. I hadn't had enough caffeine yet today to deal with this, so it was best to abandon him before I said something I shouldn't.

"By all means stick around if you want to. Feel free to search for hidden solar farms, but you won't find any." I called over my shoulder as I headed around to the back of the house to put the kettle on again. "But stay away from the wobbly walls, they're dangerous. I'd hate for you to get squashed!"

With that I put him from my mind and stalked back indoors to recharge my cup and my hidden hot water bottle.

4: Juggernaut

Definition: Huge powerful, overwhelming force or large heavy vehicle, especially an articulated lorry.

Still in the past...

Ten minutes later I was back on the drive with more tea, relieved to find that Grumpy Van Man was gone. No sooner had I settled back on my little bench seat I registered an unusual noise. Quite a loud noise and one that was getting louder all the time, in all honesty I could actually feel this particular noise too. The very ground under my feet started to tremble and so did the bench beneath my bottom. I looked nervously at my wobbly cottage walls as the intensely vibrating noise got closer and closer.

'What next?' I asked myself. For a quiet country lane it was all go this morning. I was about to struggle to my feet again to investigate the disturbance (with this many clothes on any sudden movement is impaired considerably) but before I could do so a large vehicle hove into sight at the entrance to the drive. It was enormous. I wasn't even sure exactly what was going on, but it would appear that the largest lorry on the planet had just arrived outside my house.

I wondered several things simultaneously. Things like: Had the driver seriously not spotted the two large 'not appropriate for heavy goods vehicles' signs at the turning onto this lane? And 'How on earth had they actually made it through the ford at the far end of the road?' There were other questions that sprang to mind, but the one I was most interested in was how exactly he was planning to get that humungous thing out again? After all he couldn't very well leave it parked outside my house now could he? If that were an option, then believe me our static caravan would be located right there and not in our garden so that Beloved Husband would not have had to mourn the loss of such a large section of his hedge last year. (He still hasn't got over it!)

Guessing correctly that this probably wasn't our much longed for building team either, I stood up as quickly as my multiple layers would allow and wandered casually over as the colossal cabin door swung open. A small shaggy-looking, male figure emerged. His face was bug-eyed with tiredness. The stale, rumpled air of someone who has been driving for far too many hours without a break, hung off him like a badly fitting coat.

Between you and me, he looked far too young to be in charge of such an enormous piece of equipment (no dodgy metaphor intended). But then everyone looks too young to me these days, paramedics, policemen and now juggernaut drivers. Not that I had ever seen one of the latter before. I had always assumed that such people were somewhat similarly proportioned to the vehicles they drive.

It would seem not.

I watched as the slender, dishevelled young man slithered to the ground and sat on the footplate looking dazed and exhausted. Maybe the shock of trying to negotiate the icy ford followed by a hairpin bend in such an outsized mode of transport will do that to a fella. Who am I to say? I find it hard enough in a Citroen C3. Proof that size isn't everything if we ever needed it.

Anyway, the driver and I eyed each other for quite some time. At least he wasn't shouting at me like the last chap so that was an improvement.

I smiled tentatively and raised my eyebrows inquiringly at him. He nodded, sighed and shrugged.

Ok, so he was one of those. The silent type!

No matter! I had a wealth of experience of communicating with verbally challenged young men (Yes, I am thinking of my previously-silent, older son Quiet.) so I fixed this new arrival with one of my 'no-nonsense' looks.

"Hello," I said clearly. "Are you OK?"'

He shook his head sadly and sighed again.

I can't help it, the mothering instinct kicked in without me really being aware of it. He looked so exhausted, lost and young. It made me feel like inviting him in and feeding him before ringing his mother to tell her he was safe. You will be pleased to know I resisted the impulse. I had more than enough people to look after as it was without adopting any old (or young) lame ducks that happened to park their lorry outside my house.

"Are you lost?" I tried again.

He rubbed the back of his neck, and then the rather grimy stubble on his chin with a very shaky hand. Even though this really wasn't going terribly well, I persevered.

"Can I help you?" I asked. There was more head shaking.

It did occur to me to wonder if I should just hop up into the cab and attempt to move the monster vehicle far enough down the lane so my missing builders could get past it and onto my drive, (if they ever turned up that is). Then again, I thought that perhaps I should just leave this rather odd chap to sit in the road in peace and quiet for as long as he wanted to.

All of a sudden he reached into his back pocket and fished out a mobile phone.

'Great!' I thought, 'typical youngster, can't communicate with an actual person and would far rather be on some social media site than engage with a real human being.' However, contrary to appearances, it became clear that he wasn't on Facebook or snap-chatting with his mates about the strange lady he had just found standing next to a crumbling old cottage in the deepest darkest countryside. He started speaking into the handset in rapid ... um... well I didn't actually know what it was. All I knew was that it sounded vaguely eastern European and I definitely didn't understand it.

Then to my alarm he handed the phone to me.

I looked at it as if he was trying to hand me a grenade.

I should point out here that I have always had a life-long issue with telephones. I absolutely hate them. Texting I can do. Even e-mailing is fine, but talking on a telephone? Not so much. It's got something to do with not being able to see the other person's face. I find I turn into my older son, Quiet, on the phone and start shrugging, which isn't terribly useful. I never say the right thing and I always feel that I am missing the main gist of the conversation; all potentially relevant verbal responses fall straight out of the back of my head never to be heard of again.

Looking at the handset in horror I tentatively reached out for it, almost as if I expected it to bite me at any moment. I put it to my ear wondering what hope I had of successful communication with a complete stranger in an unidentified foreign language.

“Hello?” I said cautiously.

“Allo,” crackled a cheerful voice from what seemed like a thousand miles away.

OK that was a good start! I felt ridiculously emboldened by this minor success. We had greeted each other in spite of the potential pit falls of my telephone phobia, an undisclosed distance and an unidentified language. I didn’t know who I was talking to, where they were or even why I was talking to them. Nevertheless I was rather intrigued as to what would happen next.

“Wayit pliz!” Cheerful Voice said.

OK, I thought, I could wait. I looked at the lorry driver but he merely shrugged again before inspecting his tatty trainers.

I could hear some sort of a scratchy conversation going on in the background of wherever my new telephone pal was and then all of a sudden he was back. “Ewe spik German?” he demanded.

I contemplated my thirty year old German GCSE result for a second before answering "No!" very firmly indeed. Even though I had successfully scraped through that particular language exam, I was pretty certain that the extensive German vocabulary I had swotted up on to describe what I did on my holiday in 1985 was not going to be terribly useful for any 'moving a lost juggernaut on a country lane' issues three decades plus later.

"OK. Wayit...." there was another pause before he continued hopefully, "Polish?"

"No chance."

"Russian?" Cheerful Voice's cheerful voice was gaining a slightly impatient edge now.

Seriously?

Was this just some big hoax to make me feel linguistically inferior?

Employing the entirety of my Russian language repertoire, I replied "Nyet" very clearly.

There was a sigh from the other end of the phone as if Cheerful Voice thought I was being most inconsiderate and unhelpful.

As we seemed to be playing some sort of language one-upmanship here, I felt like suggesting Welsh or Icelandic as options. I had spent 15 years in Wales as a child and acquired not only the ability to put on a strong Valleys accent but also an extensive collection of colourful expletives including the ability to ask politely where the toilet was in slightly imperfect Welsh. None of which would be terribly helpful here but, still, it was another language to throw into the pot!

Added to that there was the 'learn-to-speak Icelandic' tape I remembered my dad listening to nearly four decades before, but, as I didn't think that would prove particularly constructive either, I kept quiet.

There was more muted discussion in the background. The sleepy-looking lorry driver continued to contemplate his feet, although I was beginning to wonder if he had actually nodded off.

Feeling fairly inadequate now, I ambled down the (not inconsiderable) length of the vehicle as I waited to find out what other languages they would like to know that I didn't speak. Come to think of it, it was a fairly extensive list. Chinese, Mandarin, Urdu? And many, many more... We could be here all day!

"Français?" Cheerful asked with a certain amount of disgust in his tone. Obviously he was not keen on French as a method of communication.

"Mais, bien sûr, Monsieur!" I answered him with studied nonchalance. At last! A language I stood half a chance of blagging my way through. I continued very casually, "Je parle français, pas de problème!" I didn't want to let on that I hadn't used my French language skills since I'd burned my A-level notes twenty seven years previously, following a mortifying U in the French literature paper that brought my overall grade down from a comfortable B to an extremely embarrassing D. Especially as that particular paper had been the only one written and answered entirely in English! (But let's not go there! Some things are best forgotten.)

As I could be fairly certain that Cheerful wasn't about to launch into a detailed discussion on the literary merits of Le Comte de Monte-Cristo verses Les Liaisons Dangereuses over the telephone, I felt it was pretty safe for me to dust off my decades old French language skills.

It turned out Cheerful wasn't a French expert either. In fact I wouldn't be exaggerating particularly if I said that my French was vastly superior to his, although this really wasn't much of an achievement. In the meantime, I had been wandering along looking at the sides of the huge vehicle while we spoke and I thought I knew where my tired truck driver was trying to go.

Cheerful murdered several sentences in French which proved entertainingly incomprehensible. Nevertheless I replied "Oui!" encouragingly several times before the jumble of mashed phrases he used included two words in particular "ferme" (farm) and "solaire" (solar). Putting these clues together with the pictures on the side of the lorry I concluded that my lorry driver was attempting to get to the very same solar farm as my earlier visitor Grumpy Van Man. No doubt this mega-transporter was carrying the very solar panels that Grumpy had been enlisted to install. So he was right all along, I did have his solar panels – ho hum!

Thank goodness the juggernaut was facing the right way so there would be no need to try to turn him around. His route from here on would be simple, if I could only persuade him to get back in the cab and start the engine.

"OK!" I interrupted Cheerful's tidal wave of 'almost' French. "C'est simple. Vous allez tout droit pour trois kilomètres," I said firmly if not entirely correctly. "Bien, vous êtez arrivés a la ferme solaire." (Basically, as I've already mentioned, I told him that the solar farm was a bit further down the road.)

I handed the phone back to its owner, who took it reluctantly and listened to Cheerful translate my directions from French into whatever language he understood. There was a fairly lengthy, unintelligible argument between the two, but I rather felt I had done my bit so I waited patiently for him to accept the inevitable and go away.

Then the tired lorry driver looked at me suspiciously several times but I simply smiled and nodded encouragingly, whilst pointing down the road. Then he sighed heavily before shoving the phone back in his pocket, hauling himself up into the huge cabin and starting the engine. Without so much as a nod of thanks my way he slammed the door shut and hauled his huge lorry off in the direction of the solar farm. There's gratitude for you!

Quite frankly, Tired and Grumpy were welcome to each other.

I sat back down on my bench before concluding that it had been a long morning already and it was definitely time for me to find some breakfast.

5: Alchemy

Definition: medieval chemistry based on attempts to transform base metals into gold.

Returning to the present 'me' sitting on the bench on the drive, over two years later...

Having finished my cup of tea, whilst contemplating the past, I realised that I still really needed a sugar hit. Chaos and Logic's goodie-baking habits were proving to have been far more addictive than I had ever realised. Having freshly baked cookies and cake on tap all the time is a hard thing to learn to do without. It's almost as bad as the girls leaving home in the first place, followed by me belatedly realising that I was the only female left behind.

It had taken a while to sink in, but now it was official! The family's two resident bakers had both left home. I was completely bemused as to who was going to sustain our not insignificant sugar habit and tried to brush off the seriousness of the situation. 'It'll do us good to go without so many sweet things in our diet,' I had thought initially, 'we'll be fine.'

Ha!

Wrong!

It only took ten days for me to realise my mistake! Ten days of the sulks (Yes, me, not the boys!); I blamed my bad behaviour on a combination of low blood sugar and seeing Facebook and Snapchat photos of the cakes and cookies that were now being made for new student-flat friends.

Traitors!

In desperation, two weeks after my girls left home, I had decided to try and dust off my dormant biscuit-making skills.

"It can't be that hard," I told myself, "I used to do this all the time. Anyway, who on earth taught them to bake in the first place?"

We should note here that I was conveniently forgetting that it was my mother-in-law and also my mother who had both been quite active in educating my darling daughters in the fine art of baking. I am generally way better at savouries, than sweets.

You can take my word for it. Baking is not at all like riding a bike. It is entirely possible to forget how to do it, and it soon became apparent that I had successfully done just that. What followed was a series of batches of slightly soggy shortbread and several dangerously depressed cakes, but on the whole the flapjacks looked quite good. At least, they did, until I tried to take them out of the tin. Fortunately the boys didn't seem to mind, they demolished all my seriously, sub-standard offerings with impressive speed. It's all sugar after all isn't it?

Eventually I had given in and started buying in biscuits and cakes but they weren't the same. Fresh home baked produce is far more satisfying than the highly preserved, packet variety on sale in most supermarkets. A small portion of one of my girls' lovely fresh cakes was a treat that filled me up, whereas shop bought cake just left me feeling unsatisfied and looking round for more sugar.

Unfortunately, while I was quite capable of throwing together hearty and healthy savoury dishes, my baking skills left a lot to be desired. As my mum always says, practice makes perfect. Hmm, quite a lot more practice was needed it would seem, but never mind.

No time like the present then...

'Right,' I thought pulling myself together and heading for the kitchen, 'I am a strong independent woman! I can bake, it's easy.'

However as I dived into the kitchen cupboards in search of ingredients, successfully emerging sometime later with a scraggy bag of sugar, some ancient oats and some long forgotten raisins, I knew that the skill required to transform these basic ingredients into something of significantly more edible value might well be beyond me. It looked like flapjacks might potentially be on the horizon if only I could locate some butter somewhere.

While I was amassing useful baking related paraphernalia, like scales, bowls and wooden spoons, on the kitchen surface the IPad started to bleep at me indicating an incoming Skype call.

One positive aspect that had come from my girl Barbarians leaving was that it had forced me to be a bit more technologically minded. Chaos had set me up a profile on Facebook with a group chat so that we could stay in touch and Logic had demonstrated some of the finer points of Skype, which meant that I was able to accept incoming calls from both girls at the same time and we could all chat together. Get me! Just call me a tech queen!

Flipping the IPad open I accepted the call and couldn't help but smile when I saw Logic grinning back at me.

"Hi there! Hang on just a mo, Chaos should be joining us any minute now!" she said, "Hey, are you baking?"

Before I could answer her, the screen flickered ominously and I thought I was going to lose the connection. An incoming call registered and I accepted it; then all of a sudden the picture split and Chaos appeared.

"Hiya!" she said, "wow, are you baking?"

"I can bake you know," I said defensively, suddenly tempted to turn my IPad camera off so they couldn't see what I was doing.

There was an almost infinitesimal pause before Logic said soothingly, "Of course you can!"

"We know that!" insisted Chaos rather too firmly.

There was another pause.

"So!" She continued, "What are you making?"

I looked at the sorry looking pile of random ingredients. Casting around quickly I spotted the tail end of some butter lurking by the bread bin, obviously waiting for someone to clear it away after breakfast (like that was ever going to happen) and grabbed it quickly.

"Flapjacks!" I said triumphantly.

"That's cool," replied Logic. "Have you remembered to put the oven on to warm up?"

"I know what I am doing," I said, although I hadn't remembered of course, but there was no way she could know that for certain. "So how's university going then?"

They both tumbled over each other to tell me what was going on in their lives and I smiled contentedly as I listened and measured out my ingredients. It wasn't perfect, but it was almost like having them back at home with me, sat around the breakfast bar like we used to, with a cuppa having a chat.

I heard all about their lectures and flat mates as well as the cute guy Logic had met the day before at the university sports hall. Chaos updated me on the latest book she was writing and promised to send me a draft to read through. (During all that time she had spent in hospital recovering from that emergency operation, just before the house fell down, she had started writing teen fiction. The stories were full of attitude, action and adventure, so I could see why she now had a growing following of adoring teen/tween fans all clamouring for the next book to be published.)

It was just like old times chatting away to them both and I soon forgot how lonely and lost I had been feeling.

Unfortunately it couldn't last and real life eventually interrupted our glorious gossiping session. Soon Chaos had to go to a lecture and signed off, followed a few minutes later by Logic.

"Bye," she said, "and remember, put the oven on." With a cheeky wave she was gone too. Both girls had dived back into their exciting new lives leaving me standing alone in an empty, echoing house. I stood and looked at the blank screen for a few minutes before going over to switch the oven on ready for my flapjacks.

I usually find that baking is a bit like painting, although for me the paintings generally have a much greater success rate these days. Regardless of the outcome I find both activities very relaxing. So as I slung oats, sugar and butter together in the present, grateful to have reconnected, however briefly, with my two gorgeous girls, my mind drifted back to the arrival of our superhero builders in the past.

PART 2

A Journey of a thousand miles begins with a single step

Lao Tsu
(604 BC – 531 BC)

6: Synthesis

Definition: the process of mixing constituent elements or different things into a single/cohesive object.

Back to waiting on the drive in the past....

Having successfully raided the biscuit tin in the kitchen, I had returned to the driveway yet again just as my third lot of visitors of the morning arrived. At precisely 9.25 a battered, blue van coasted onto the drive and three laughing men spilled out. A more disparate group you couldn't hope to meet but I wasn't complaining. After my earlier two arrivals, I took the fact that this lot were smiling as a very positive sign.

The driver sauntered over to me and I noticed that the closer he got the further up I had to look. He was immensely tall. "Sorry we're late," he rumbled down at me from an impressively lofty height as he jerked his head in the direction of one of his companions. "He forgot his hammer so we had to go back for it."

A more medium-sized gentleman, beautifully sun-tanned, sporting a full beard and long blonde hair held back from his face with a red bandana, stepped forward swinging a large sledgehammer from fist to fist in a surprisingly unthreatening way. (That takes some skill.) This Thor-wannabe smiled and said "Good morning." The third gentleman was tiny, probably a junior apprentice or maybe a work experience student. He was very young and hung back behind Thor. I think he was shy. Nevertheless he nodded perfectly politely at me. Another verbally challenged young man it would seem – what is it with the youth of today? (Oh dear – now I sound like my grandmother.)

"So!" continued Lofty, looking around hopefully. "Is The Boss here yet?"

"The Boss?" I queried.

It must be remembered that Beloved Husband and I had had absolutely no control over which building firm had been awarded the contract for the repair. That decision had been entirely made by the Insurance Company and communicated to us via Loss Adjuster Number Two. He was the professional representing the house insurance company and had liaised with Genuine Old Buildings Expert, who was the appointed structural engineer for the project, in establishing what work would be done. Between them they had determined which building firm was appointed.

Not surprisingly the Insurance Company had awarded the contract for the work to the firm that submitted the cheapest quote, but Genuine Old Buildings Expert had assured me that they were a very professional firm and were definitely qualified for this sort of complicated job. Nevertheless Beloved Husband and I only had a very vague idea as to who was actually going to pitch up today, although the owner of the firm (The Boss) had kindly telephoned us and introduced himself after the decision on the contract was announced.

"Don't worry! He'll be here with the structural engineer to get us off to a good start. It's important that we approach these sorts of projects in the right way," continued Lofty.

The decision, made by the insurance company, had been to not demolish the whole cob section of the cottage and rebuild it, but to prop up the roof and simply repair the two disintegrating cob walls by taking them down in stages and then rebuilding from the ground up. Now you won't be able to persuade me that supporting a massively heavy thatched roof on a few steel poles and then knocking down the walls beneath and rebuilding them is a normal 'every day' job for anyone. Or even that it is terribly safe but as I said, I wasn't the one making the decisions round here. I was also not going to be hanging around under the propped up roof for any length of time.

I planned on staying a safe distance away. Someone had to be alive to dial 999 for an ambulance if it all came crashing down didn't they?

The structural engineering team had checked the roof very carefully only recently and concluded that it had not been adversely effected by the disintegration of the two supporting walls beneath it. Genuine Old Buildings Expert had assured me that the remaining solid wall structures plus some very key industrial props were sharing the weight of the roof extremely effectively. He had personally devised the proposed repair program about to be implemented and assured me that it would effectively fix the problem. I had no choice but to bow to his superior knowledge as he really did seem to know what he was talking about.

Nevertheless, I was rather glad when The Boss and Genuine Old Buildings Expert arrived to oversee the start of the job. Genuine Old Buildings Expert always made me feel that he was completely in control of things and it was a pleasant surprise to realise that I recognised The Boss. Wrapped up against the cold in an expensive, long woollen coat, thick scarf and leather gloves, smart trousers and shoes, he looked very different from the last time I had seen him, dressed as he was then, in a grubby boiler suit and yellow hard hat with accompanying head torch as he was about to scramble into my damaged home through a side window.

He happened to be the only builder who had actually acknowledged that Beloved Husband and I existed during the whole depressing 'quoting-for-the-rebuild-job phase' of this riveting tale. The really nice one! The one who seemed to sympathise with our situation and asked us what we would like to do with the house if we got the chance. All the other prospective building firms had ignored us completely and concentrated on communicating directly with the insurance company.

You will probably agree, in the light of this development, that we were off to a rather good start. I could feel myself starting to believe that this just might work after all.

So having greeted these two new arrivals with genuine delight I set off for the kitchen to make the first of a great many rounds of tea while they all had a pow-wow about where to start.

Shortly afterwards The Boss came round to the patio door and said, 'We have a slight problem.'

My heart sank.

Already? They've only been here twenty minutes!

"Don't worry!" he continued, "we can sort it out, but would you like to come and see, and I'll explain what needs to be done and why."

Wow! Inclusion, with information! Yes I would definitely like to come and see.

It seems that the insurance's re-build plan which relied so heavily on the roof being propped up had also relied on there being a solid concrete floor for the propping equipment to rest on. Unfortunately our three hundred and fifty year old cottage didn't have a concrete floor of any description, solid or otherwise, which was something that hadn't come to light until just now, when our new builders dug a small exploratory hole to check.

It would seem that we had been living here for nearly fourteen years not knowing that our beautiful 1970's wooden parquet flooring was laid directly on to compacted earth. It was in remarkably good condition under the circumstances – well apart from the sections that had been damaged by the collapsing walls, oh and the bits that had got wet near the cracks where the rain had got in, but other than that it was fine. Unfortunately it wasn't going to be strong enough to support the weight of the first floor and the roof as planned.

"There's quite an easy solution really," said The Boss smoothly, "we're going to have to bring in some large steel girders to lie across the floor in place of the concrete slab that was supposed to be here. Then the propping plan can go ahead as before. It's just going to take a little time to get them here. There's a bit of prep work we can do in the meantime but we can't really get going till the steels are in place. Sorry!"

Please don't say they are leaving? I think I might cry!

"We can get them here late this afternoon with any luck. Is that ok?"

Phew! Tearful deluge averted.

"Sure," I said trying not to sound too relieved. With our luck I had thought they were going to say they would be back in six weeks! We'd been waiting so long, another half day I could cope with but I don't think I could bear to see them leave at this point. So late this afternoon was good!

7: Infusion

Definition: a remedy or solution created by soaking the leaves of a plant or herb in a liquid

Returning to the present...

Having thoroughly mixed up the flapjack ingredients while I thought back over that first day of building work, I now shoved the tray of oats, sugar and butter into the oven to cook and started back to my studio to carry on with my abandoned painting. On the way there though, my attention was caught by another canvas. Unusually, this particular piece of work hadn't been hastily stuffed out of the way as was my normal habit with finished canvases.

Beloved Husband had taken a bit of a shine to it and had appropriated it before I could shove it in one of the sheds. As a result it now adorned the wall in the hallway near the front door. The Barbarians seemed to be quite fond of it too which surprised me as I had been going through a very dark phase of guilt when I'd painted it last year so in some ways it is quite menacing. It has a deep, Prussian blue acrylic base that was applied in a frantic rush using a roller from the DIY store. Over that I had used silver to pick out the highlights of a lone lady surfer riding a massive curling and crashing wave.

Looking at it now, I supposed that it really represented the resilience of human beings overcoming the immense power of nature and surviving in spite of the danger around them, which could probably be considered very meaningful given what had happened to us. Anyway, I shrugged the thought away and carried on to my studio and my new canvas.

Restoration

This was also going to be a fairly big painting. I had found a large, old, canvas board lurking at the back of my wardrobe. I have no idea what it was doing there. Perhaps I had bought it and then felt guilty at the expense (the big ones can be quite pricey) so hidden it for a bit and then forgotten about it.

It's a bit like when you buy a new dress or shoes or something but don't like to admit you've spent quite that much so you put them in your wardrobe for a few weeks before actually wearing them in public. Then when your Beloved Husband says "Is that new?" you can legitimately say dismissively "What this old thing? It's been in the wardrobe for *ages*!"

The sensible husband makes no comment at that point, other than to say, "You look lovely, dear." He knows what you are doing and you know he knows but honour is satisfied. Or at least an unpleasant disagreement is avoided which is just as important. It's also far too late by then to return the items for a refund so you have to keep them.

Devious? Not at all. Merely practical!

Anyway I had liberated the re-discovered canvas board and made use of it. As always when stressed I reverted to painting fish. These paintings are all different, but still have the same innate message of hope and positivity as the fish spiral up out of the deep dark depths of the ocean towards the light breaking through the surface of the water.

Usually, I found the process of painting my little silver fish immensely soothing although Quiet had taken to commenting tactfully (or not!) "Why on earth are you painting more fish? Are you obsessed or something?" I generally ignored these remarks. For a mild-mannered chap, he'd been a bit irritable lately. I put it down either to hormones or the fact that he was actually missing his sisters. Not that he'd admit to either factor of course.

I don't know what he was worried about though! These paintings were really popular. The imagery was representative of 'the light at the end of the tunnel' and was very uplifting. People were always asking to buy them from me to give as gifts which made me confident that they would sell well if I ever got around to exhibiting them. So it wasn't as if we were collecting a huge pile of useless fish paintings or anything – well - apart from the fact that I hadn't arranged an exhibition recently so the pile was growing steadily.....

OK, maybe he had a point!

Probably due to my agitation after the road accident that morning and then the arrival of the For Sale sign, this new piece of work was a rather more energetic painting than previous versions. Done in traditional oil paints I had applied paint in fat lines directly onto the canvas board straight from the tube and then blended using a large rounded palette knife. Thick swirls of Prussian green, morphed upwards from the bottom left corner, through phthalo turquoise, French ultramarine to cerulean blue and on into sparkling titanium white at the top right hand corner. Such fun! Messy but so exhilarating to paint! The oils were going to take a very long time to dry completely but I didn't care about that. I never did when I was immersed in a piece of work. I also didn't mind that I was wearing rather a lot of paint too. It was almost as if I had become part of the canvas for a time.

Now the ocean component of the piece was complete it was time to add the fish. Payne's Grey and silver smoothed into the thick shades of green and blue using a smaller palette knife to create each shape. This critical phase required absolute concentration and precision to get the right effect. The larger fish at the base of the painting weren't a problem but when it came to the smaller ones further up I started to struggle.

The canvas was quite big, so I looked around for a small stool to stand on. My thinking was that if I could reach the upper section more easily, then perhaps all would be fine.

Unfortunately it wasn't that simple.

I lost count of the number of times I approached the canvas with my sharp knife loaded with silver paint, ready for the quick sweeping action that would bring my little fish to life in the rippling water, only to have to stop short because I couldn't control the distinct tremor in my hands.

You would be forgiven for thinking that I was in some sort of delayed shock given the eventful morning I had experienced. In a way you would be right, but it was unfortunately more profound than that. This was happening more and more these days! I had tried to ignore it but it wasn't going away. It would seem that I had developed a significant and uncontrollable trembling of the hands for no apparent reason.

I didn't think there was anything physically wrong with me. I actually felt fine – well - it's all relative isn't it? Let me put it this way, I didn't feel as rubbish as I had previously when I had been consumed with guilt over not being able to protect the Barbarians from the house falling down. I was much better than I had been then, but this persistent shaking was getting concerning. Beloved Husband had tentatively suggested a number of times that I ought to consider going to see my GP about it. It's not that bad, though, I was sure it would settle down in time. No need to waste the good doctor's time, or my own, come to think of it.

I tried one more time to complete the smaller fish but it was no good. Bizarrely, I found that concentrating hard on keeping my hands steady made the tremor seem even more pronounced. Finally, snarling in frustration, I flung the knife down, heedless of the silver oil paint splattering everywhere, turned on my heels and left the room.

I headed straight for the kettle. Switching it on forcefully, I lifted my prized teapot off the shelf and reached for the caddy of real tealeaves, hoping that the action of making proper tea in a proper pot would calm me down.

As the kettle came to the boil I noticed the smoke coming from the oven. Sighing heavily, I swiftly extracted the cremated flapjacks, dumping them on the draining board, before concentrating on warming the pot thoroughly and then making my tea. With a loaded tray containing the teapot, a cup (with saucer – let's do this properly), and a milk jug I headed back outside to sit on my bench on the drive, hoping to calm down in the beautiful sunshine.

The next twenty minutes saw me work my way through at least four cups of tea. At the same time I let the warm sunshine wash over me soothing my nerves and calming me down. I was pretty certain that the tremor was probably just an annoying legacy from the most bizarre period of my life, the physical manifestation of delayed stress. Perhaps an over-reaction of my fight or flight response, no doubt brought on as a result of living under the immense anxiety associated with having a falling-down-house for such a long period of time.

There had been other more cosmetic consequences too. I have heard it suggested that the lines on your face can tell the story of your life and that one should be proud of them, not try to conceal them. By that measure I should be full to the brim with pride! Believe me, I am not particularly. In my case I felt that every second of the time that we lived in our garden had been chiselled into my face in bold italics and underlined twice for good measure.

Not to mention the striking silver (ok grey) streak that now adorned my head for all to see. I am not joking, I woke up one morning, soon after we had moved back into our home, to find that the minor sprinkling of grey hairs, that I had been kidding myself were little blond highlights, had migrated overnight to congregate in one place, just above my right temple, forming a wide grey streak that no amount of home dye could hide.

No matter how much I tried to laugh about all these changes, I couldn't ignore the fact that my shaking hands were seriously starting to interfere with my art and things would only go downhill if I couldn't paint.

Sitting there in the warm sunshine and trying to relax, I became aware of that sensation of light-headedness again. It was quite bizarre. I could hear the blood rushing in my ears and feel my heartbeat thumping loudly in my head. Then all of a sudden the thumping seemed to stop.

I know we are not normally aware of our own heartbeat, but there was a long pause in which I definitely knew that my heart wasn't beating at all. Something similar had happened several times over recent weeks but those previous episodes had passed relatively quickly.

This time it wasn't passing quickly at all.

Time seemed to slow right down as I gasped for breath.

What on earth was happening?

All of a sudden the thumping resumed as my heart seemed to crash back into play but this time the systematic rhythm was all wrong. It felt off-kilter, as if it was missing beats out or trying to beat on something that wasn't there.

I blinked rapidly as I tried to stay calm, not really succeeding. A panic attack right now really wasn't going to help things. I tried to think what to do but my mind went blank. All I could hear was my own rapid, gasping breathing as the seconds dragged by. Was I having a heart attack?

Was I going to die?

Sat outside my cottage in the middle of nowhere?

On my own?

I had rather pinned my hopes on a moving, yet peaceful, deathbed scene in my late nineties, surrounded by my children and hundreds of grand and great grandchildren. So dying now, on the driveway, without an audience, would be somewhat disappointing!

Just as my brain formulated that irreverent thought I became aware of the fact that my funny heartbeat had returned to normal. The rushing sound in my ears subsided. The light-headedness started to clear and I could once again hear the birds singing in the hedgerow and the drone of a passing bumble bee.

My breathing started to ease and my shoulders relaxed.

What on earth had happened? I don't know how long I sat there feeling dizzy and faintly nauseous but eventually I came to the galling conclusion that Beloved Husband was probably right. (How annoying!) I was going to have to pay a visit to the doctor.

When I was certain that all of the weird sensations had stopped, I slowly gathered up the tea things, including a large white feather that had somehow found its way onto the tray, headed back inside and reached for the telephone. A short while later I found myself in proud possession of an appointment to see my doctor the next day; which was nothing short of a minor miracle. Normally, the doctors at the local surgery are so over-worked that you have to wait ages to see anyone at all. So getting an appointment with the one specific doctor you would prefer within twenty-four hours is unheard of. Apparently I was in luck and there had been a cancellation just minutes before I telephoned.

Still feeling somewhat dazed and shaky I rummaged under the sink to find a cloth so I could clean up the dramatic spray of silver oil paint in the studio before it became a permanent feature on my nice new wooden flooring and beautifully rebuilt cottage walls.

****

The next afternoon, I found myself being called into the doctor's consulting room after a surprisingly short interval in the hot and stuffy waiting room. There was some sort of children's clinic on at the same time so lots of mothers had brought their darling offspring along to share bugs and scrap over the sparse, grubby and somewhat battered, old Fisher Price toys provided. A mere ten minutes in that overcrowded space with so many small children gave me a fairly stark reminder of what it was like to live with toddlers again and I could feel myself beginning to re-evaluate quite how much I missed that period of my life!

Gratefully leaving the scene of mayhem behind me, I shuffled nervously into the consulting room, closed the door and sat gingerly on the edge of the chair provided. I don't really know why I was nervous because my GP is lovely, even though she was looking decidedly tired and harassed. I didn't blame her. I'd seen what was in the waiting room and that was probably only a small snippet of what she had on her plate to sort out that day. I was beginning to wish I hadn't bothered her.

Now I am sure I have mentioned my opinion of people discussing their health issues before. It is a subject that has the potential to be very boring and I don't intend to start banging on about my own problems here. Suffice to say it is unfortunately a necessary part of this storyline and therefore I will sum up what went on in the doctor's consulting room as concisely as possible.

Obviously I mentioned the funny turns I'd experienced and my history of persistent trembling. The doctor, stifling a yawn, pulled a blood test form out of a drawer and started to fill it in while asking about any recent stresses. I briefly mentioned that the house had fallen down and that we had spent over a year living in the garden with the children while we rebuilt it and that the house was now on the market. This information certainly got her attention and she looked significantly more interested. I didn't mention my almost permanent headache or the recurrent nightmare I was having that featured the staircase disintegrating beneath me and an awful sensation of falling. I felt that the psychiatrists would have a field day with that one, hence it was best avoided. Some things just don't need sharing.

Inevitably the question of low mood and anxiety came up and a prescription was offered and politely refused. Whether this was a wise decision or not on my part I couldn't possibly say, I just know I hate taking tablets. I agreed with the doctor that I had probably been depressed the year before but that had since improved; it was merely the recent development of physical symptoms which worried me. What followed was quite an enlightening discussion on the fact that on-going stress and high anxiety can manifest in some very real physical symptoms, so whilst my mood had lifted the rest of me was struggling to follow. The pressure of living under such difficult circumstances had potentially left me with a physical legacy that my body was trying to recover from and it was up to me to give it the best chance of doing that by looking after myself. It certainly seemed logical the way she explained it.

The upshot of the whole consultation was that I was to have some tests on my heart to rule out any major problems but she didn't anticipate any being identified. Then she gave me a gentle but firm lecture on self-care; recommended that I give up caffeine, reduce my refined sugar intake, avoid alcohol because it interferes with both mood and sleep patterns and finally, I was to get some exercise.

So no major surprises there then.

"You might also consider making sure you socialise a bit more. If you miss your daughters so much, go and join some ladies groups. Get some female company that way. There are plenty around; book groups, lunch clubs, the Women's Institute. Take your pick." She grinned and handed me the blood test form as she said this.

"So will all this get rid of the shaking so I can paint?" I asked, getting to the root of what I was really worrying about. (I know; I am obsessed.)

"Well, art can be a very powerful therapy and you must definitely keep painting if you find it so helpful. I am sure you can adapt the way you paint to work around the tremor if you put your mind to it. But the really important thing is that you start to put your general health higher up on your priority list. I know you are a busy mum and that you have a job as well. But that's no excuse for not taking care of yourself. If *you* don't do it, no-one else will." She said rather bluntly and then muttered, "We mothers are allowed to put ourselves first occasionally, you know!"

Whether she was talking to me or herself at that point I wasn't too sure.

Gathering up my blood form and bag, I smiled, said goodbye and retreated back out into the corridor trying not to trip over any toddlers as I crossed the waiting room. Tiptoeing around a two year old indulging in an epic tantrum, I thanked the receptionist and headed off to visit the vampires at the local hospital to get those blood tests done.

8: Amalgamation

Definition: uniting, the bringing together of associated items that work well together or combining to create a whole.

Back to the reconstruction site in the past.....

The steels arrived, just as The Boss said they would, late that afternoon. This was almost unbelievable. It seemed that we had fallen on our feet at last. After so many months of waiting, enforced inactivity and uncertainty I was going to have to re-learn that some people are reliable and that it was possible to make forward progress.

Some time ago I received a fortune cookie that, when opened, revealed the following wise words: *you don't have to see the whole staircase to take the first step*. Under the circumstances this was good advice on two levels because theoretically speaking I had no idea how our home was actually going to be fixed and practically speaking we didn't have an operational staircase at all just then.

Speaking of which, the majority of the old, damaged staircase had been cleared out that morning by Thor with his trusty sledgehammer. The rubble had been replaced with a sturdy wooden ladder so that the construction crew could reach the first floor safely.

I watched with some satisfaction as our team of builders busied themselves installing the steels in carefully selected locations overseen by Genuine Old Building Expert. Then I observed the assembling of an intricate system of props initially lifting the weight of the first floor onto the steels laid down on the ground floor and then establishing a second series of props upstairs to take the weight of the roof on the now stabilised first floor joists.

There was much bustling around and calling out to each other and readjusting of props as they carefully ensured that what was left of our house wasn't going to move any further when they were eventually ready to go about the tricky business of taking down the remnants of the two damaged walls in order to rebuild them.

This all took place very smoothly in spite of the fact that the whole of the front of the property had previously been encased in black plastic sheets to try and keep out the worst of the weather. These sheets had been left in place for the time being with a large, upright split cut for access through the sheeting level with the largest crack in the front wall of the house. The builders were using this crack as a door as the actual door had been wedged shut by the weight of the disintegrating wall above it. The team had come fully prepared with large industrial lights and long extension cables to light up the inside of the property so that they could see what they were doing.

The Boss arrived back on site just as the team were packing up to go for the day. He checked everything over thoroughly and then said, 'It's an unusual job, of course, but the structural engineers have got everything in hand. We have worked with them on several very complicated jobs and they really do know their stuff. You are in good hands I promise. They are the geniuses behind this operation and they've worked out exactly how to do this so you don't need to worry. We are going to follow their instructions to the letter and if we hit any snags we'll just call them out to advise us.

The property is all completely stable now, so we can start taking the first wall down tomorrow.'

"Are you sure it's safe?" I asked regarding him sceptically.

"Completely! Believe me! I wouldn't put my team at risk, or you and your family. Relax. Now that all this is in place, this project can officially start. As of tomorrow we are going to begin fixing your home."

I really wanted to believe him but my faith in things being OK had been stretched rather thin over the last six months.

I think he realised how twitchy I was feeling so he continued reassuringly "Just think, you'll have proper foundations too, when we've finished. These new walls won't be going anywhere. I promise!" He turned to go but then remembered something and said, "By the way they are going to be delivering a porta-loo for the team to use while we're here. It should arrive sometime this evening. Would you mind telling them to site it over there please?" He waved vaguely in the direction of the garage before nodding to me and heading off for the day.

A porta-loo? Good idea. While the team were welcome to use the loo in the house it wasn't easily accessible for them and the one in the caravan would be tricky. I decided not to wonder where they had done their business that day. Some things you just don't need to know.

It was reassuring to know that our team of genius engineers and super-talented builders had thought of everything even down to the most basic essentials. Brilliance and common sense together in the same package! This I felt boded well for the job to come.

I understand the concept of genius. Not that I am a genius myself, of course, far from it, but I know a few of people who are pretty darn smart. As a result I am well acquainted with the fact that true genius doesn't always come hand in hand with common sense.

I came across one of my favourite genii not five minutes after I had waved goodbye to my lovely building team for the evening. When I had left her earlier to watch the fascinating propping process take place and then to chat briefly to The Boss, she had been sat at her books at the breakfast bar muttering to herself about the electron density distribution of multi-hetroatomic molecules. (No, I really don't know what that is. I had to get her to write it down so I could type it in here.) Now I returned in time to see that she was apparently having a major physical issue with something over the dustbin.

Small was leaning against the oven eating ice cream directly from the carton, like they do in American sitcoms. (Please note that it's against my house rules to eat anything straight from the carton, but it would seem that he has conveniently forgotten this fact and I couldn't summon the energy to enforce it at that particular moment. The chances were that he would eat the whole thing in one sitting anyway, so I decided to focus on the fact that there would be less washing up and let the issue slide.) He was observing his sister's unusual behaviour with mild interest but no obvious sign of alarm.

He looked across at me as I approached, momentarily distracted from his sibling's antics, and grinned rather messily around a large mouthful of mint choc chip. I raised an enquiring eyebrow at him but he merely shrugged and resumed watching the live show unfolding before us.

Chaos hastily brushed some long blond hair out of her eyes and shook the item in her hand even more violently. She gave a dramatic sigh before saying crossly, "Why do they design them like this? It's ridiculous!"

I edged a little closer to see what it was that she had in her hands. Having correctly identified the object I began to understand what was going on. Looking accusingly at Small, I sighed heavily before saying, "OK, are you going to tell her or am I?"

"Tell her what?" he said looking confused. He clearly had no idea what was going on and wasn't going to be much help.

I approached the frustrated genius myself, held out my hand and said calmly, "Give!"

"It's jammed!" she said, "they are great for a while and then they always get jammed and you can't get the stuff out. Someone should design them a bit better. I've got all this work to do," she gestured at the paperwork spread all over the kitchen counter, "I haven't got time for this." She thrust it at me and huffed.

I looked her directly in the eye and said; "Watch this!"

Then I turned the item over and carefully peeled off the plastic base allowing the compacted bits of unwanted paper to fall easily into the bin.

"Oh!" she said entranced, "Is that a thing? That's really clever." I replaced the plastic base and gave it back to her and she examined it really closely. "Brilliant! That's so simple. Thanks mum."

My little genius had been trying to empty her hole-punch by shaking the bits of paper back out the way they had gone in. So much incredible scientific intellect in one brain that there is no room to spare for small practical details.

I tried not to smile. She understands multi–hetroatomic molecules. Someone has to. I am glad it's not me. I understand hole-punches.

We all have our parts to play in life. I decided then and there that I was going to have to trust my clever structural engineers and their team of superhero builders. They seemed confident that they knew what they were doing. I didn't have a clue, so I was going to stick to what I do know and keep them well supplied with tea.

9: Tincture:

Definition: a drug made using a slight trace of something

Returning to the present again...

I was barely back in the house after my appointment with the GP and my subsequent encounter with the vampires, when the IPad alerted me to an incoming Skype call. Fumbling around with it clumsily I eventually managed to accept the call and put the kettle on at the same time.

“We’re worried about you! What’s this we hear about you going to see the doctor? What’s wrong?” Chaos’ dulcet tones filled the kitchen as a second incoming call registered. A digital image of Logic, in her pyjamas eating a slice of buttered toast, nudged Chaos’ concerned expression across to one side of the screen.

“Hang on a minute! How on earth did you two know I was going to the doctors?” I asked.

“We know everything,” Logic said ominously and then spoiled the effect by confessing, “Small saw a note about the appointment next to your handbag this morning. He told Quiet and Quiet texted us. So what did the doctor say?”

I took a second to absorb the fact that my youngest child was now colluding with his brother to rat on me to both of their older sisters. This probably meant that the boys were a bit concerned about me, so I said reassuringly, “There’s nothing to worry about. I just had a funny turn. I’ve got a bit of a wonky blood sugar. Apparently I need to cut out caffeine and refined sugar and get out a bit more, meet some people, do some exercise. That's all. I am fine." I crossed my fingers, not admitting to the upcoming hospital tests. There was no way they knew about those and I would make sure I didn't leave the appointment letters lying around when they arrived so that my resident Sherlock Holmes and Dr Watson couldn't snitch on me.

"I'm not surprised your blood sugar is shot to bits if you are eating that rubbish!" said Logic with a sniff. I followed her gaze and realised that she had spotted half a packet of shop bought biscuits on the kitchen counter. "Cutting those out for a start will make you feel much better."

Damn! I'd forgotten that they could see what I was doing.

"So are you going to do as you are told?" Chaos prompted.

I hadn't really decided to be honest, I was still trying to process everything the doctor had said, but I wasn't daft enough to let my girls know that.

"Of course I am." I said, grabbing the offending packet, sweeping it into the bin, just as the kettle clicked off with a noisy 'ping' indicating that it had finished boiling.

"OK, that's good!" Chaos continued, "So is that a decaf tea you are making now?"

"Ummm! Not exactly, I've only just got back from the doctor's and I am gasping for a cuppa. I haven't had a chance to go shopping yet." Truth be told, I wasn't keen on the whole decaf option. I had vaguely been thinking of just cutting back a bit and perhaps not having quite as many strong cups of coffee and tea a day.

"Mum!" the girls' amplified joint reaction informed me that I clearly wasn't going to be allowed to get away with that.

"But I am going shopping this afternoon. I will buy some decaf tea and coffee then. I promise. OK?"

"OK! Good." Chaos smiled and nodded, so I foolishly thought I was off the hook for a second. Oh no! She simply took a deep breath and then continued. "Now the other thing we wanted to talk to you about is that Quiet said you haven't really been eating proper meals lately. He says that even though you cook supper as usual, you never sit down to eat with them in the evenings these days. Why?"

"Oh, I'm just not very hungry." I replied vaguely. I could hardly tell my girls the truth, which was that I couldn't bear to look at their empty chairs at the table during meal times; the spaces where they used to sit. It was a bit pathetic really, and I genuinely hadn't realised that the boys had noticed that I wasn't joining them. They always seem in such a hurry to get back to whatever computer game supper had inadvertently interrupted.

"That's not a good thing Mum," said Chaos. "Promise us you'll try to look after yourself a bit better. It's supposed to be us developing poor eating habits because we're students, not the parent left behind. We can't concentrate on our studies if we are worrying about you. So you have to sort yourself out OK? Otherwise we're going to have to come back and look after you."

"There's no need for that," I replied. "I will behave, I promise."

After a little more insistent nagging from both girls I finally got them to sign off and head for their lectures so that I could make myself that cup of tea.

Funnily enough though, I had rather gone off it by then, so I ended up sitting and looking at it for a while, thinking back over the conversation with the girls. Eventually I came to the conclusion that they were right. Enough was enough. I was going to have to accept that, regardless of any test results, I wasn't actually very well and it was beginning to affect the people I loved; including those that weren't living at home anymore. I couldn't have that. I was going to have to pull myself together and start looking after myself, which meant following the doctor's advice.

Tipping that last cup of caffeinated tea, in its entirety down the kitchen sink and setting the cup on the draining board I caught sight of the dining table in the conservatory, with its six matching chairs. Scooping off the pile of junk mail adorning it, I yanked and pulled at the mechanism until I had removed the central leaf and contracted the table-top to a smaller configuration. Then I picked up two of the chairs and put them out of sight, one in each of the girls' bedrooms. Eventually I was left with a dining table suitable for a family of four and hoped that this evening I would be able to eat a meal with my husband and two sons without focussing on how much I missed the people who were not there. I was being silly! I couldn't have my boys worrying about me, and I shouldn't miss out on mealtimes with them just because their sisters weren't home.

Enough wallowing! It was time for things to change.

On that decisive note I grabbed my bag of shopping carriers, picked up my wallet and keys and headed for the door. It was well past time to raid the supermarket for decaf coffee, herbal teas and some healthy snack options. As I stepped out of the house I nearly tripped over a basket left on the doorstep. It was stuffed with fresh seasonal vegetables still wearing a cosy coating of warm earth. It would seem that my lovely neighbour had been around to leave an offering from her amazingly prolific vegetable garden. She is very well acquainted with my inability to grow any sort of plant successfully, and is incredibly generous with her own produce. Perhaps she had decided I needed looking after too when I bumped into her at the village shop yesterday. I was going to have to give in to the inevitable and start taking care of myself so that no one else felt obliged to.

I strongly believe that there is nothing better for you than fresh organic veggies straight out of the ground so, gathering up this kind gift, I decided that I would make some healthy soup this afternoon and ensure I ate a large bowl of it to get my new self-care plan off to a good start.

But first, the supermarket was calling!

****

I had expected a lengthy wait for an appointment at the hospital after the doctor had referred me, but I was actually seen within ten days. It just goes to show that we can grumble all we like about the NHS, but when it works, it does so absolutely brilliantly.

After sitting in another packed waiting room for about twenty minutes up at the local hospital, this time surrounded by a large number of very elderly people in wheelchairs with accompanying oxygen tanks, I was called in to have my heart scan. Following that appointment, I was swept off to be fitted with a series of wires stuck to my chest. They were attached to a small box that I was instructed to wear clipped to my belt. The technician explained quite firmly that there were to be no showers for 24 hours, so I was going to pong a bit but as I had no major plans that day it didn't really matter. I returned the next day for the whole thing to be removed and then dashed home to hit the bathroom.

Approximately a week later, I received a telephone call from my GP to confirm that thankfully the tests showed nothing to be concerned about. She reassured me that I had probably been experiencing episodes of palpitations which might happen again and that while these could be quite alarming they weren't anything to worry about. She encouraged me to follow all the advice she had given me before and asked to see me again in a couple of months so that she could check how I was getting on.

After hanging up the telephone I reached for the brochure for the local leisure centre that was pinned to the notice board by the bread bin.

In my opinion it is a very brave man who gives his wife a membership to the gym for her birthday. If I were of a more suspicious mind I could, for example, think that he might be trying to tell me that I was FAT!!! Only it should be remembered that it wasn't so long ago that he was telling me I was too skinny. The pain of having to potentially send the adored Barbarians away to live with relatives rather than live indefinitely in a tent in the garden with us, had robbed me of the ability to swallow and even speak let alone eat anything.

Therefore I felt it was necessary to give him the benefit of the doubt as it was much more likely that he had realised I had a birthday coming up and he had no idea what to buy me as a gift. So when I had given him the news that I was probably not going mad or suffering from some disastrous heart defect, merely stressed and in need of a little more fresh air, exercise and significantly less, sugar, caffeine and alcohol, he dashed out and bought me a year's membership to the local leisure centre, a bottle of sugar-free lemonade and a large box of decaffeinated teabags.

I had taken the doctor's advice to mean a brisk walk and some deep breathing exercises by the sea every morning after the school run, rather than a personal return to the green goddess movement of the eighties. I had done keep fit classes before and wasn't that keen to revisit them. However I guess it's the thought that counts. So I had decided to accept the gift graciously and give it my best shot, after all I did want to feel better, I just didn't want to die of exhaustion on the way.

Carefully scanning the list of available exercise classes to identify those that didn't look like they would be too strenuous, I found myself mentally avoiding sessions called INSANITY (Do people willingly go to these things?) and BODY ATTACK (Seriously?) that were listed in the 'calorie burning' column and opted instead for classes entitled Slow Stretch and Body Balance from the low impact list instead.

There was one class called 'Play' but I wasn't fooled. It looked highly suspicious as it was held in the gym with all the weights and resistance equipment. That was surely just a soft title to lure you into a high intensity interval training workout.

Over the last few weeks I had dutifully been going to a couple of random classes a week as well as taking those brisk walks along the beach in the mornings before going to work. Unfortunately I had yet to find a class that I wanted to stick to. I had proved that I didn't really have much rhythm or co-ordination in the Zumba class and that I lacked the basic core stability required for the Body Balance class. I don't even want to mention what happened at the 'Begin to Spin' class. Some things are best just left in the past. Yet, in spite of this less than successful beginning, I planned to persevere.

Yoga sounded interesting but there were so many different types that I hadn't a clue where to start. Ashtang, Bikram, Hatha and Moksha to name but a few, then there are modified versions such as Power Yoga and Yoga Fusion, the list seemed endless. Nevertheless it was listed as a 'relax and re-energise' class rather than an 'Endurance' one so that was probably worth a go. I decided to try one of them out that evening and had bought a yoga mat from the charity shop in the village the previous week in anticipation. This just might be the exercise class for me.

Lots of serenity and calmness! Bring it on!

10: Re-energise

Definition: to give renewed vitality and enthusiasm.

Staying with the stressed out mother in the present...

That evening, as soon as I had collected the boy Barbarians from school and given them their tea, I changed into my gym kit determined not to back out of my plan to try Yoga.

I must confess that I did fuss about a bit first before leaving. I told Quiet that he was in charge until Beloved Husband got home from work in half an hour and then reminded him twice to make sure that if anything bad happened, like the house falling down again, he and Small were just to get outside to safety as quickly as they could and then to phone me ASAP.

I do not deny that I am still paranoid! Lightening can strike twice you know. I am just rather hoping it won't.

Eventually, Quiet said, in his not-so-quiet-now voice, "For goodness sake mother, just go will you?" Or words to that effect! He's a teenage boy, so I have no idea what he actually said, but I got his general meaning and therefore sped off in my muddy, little, purple car towards the gym and my very first yoga class.

On reflection I probably should have taken the time to check that I had been looking at an up to date class timetable. But I didn't. Had I done so, my evening would no doubt have been very different.

Restoration

A warning bell potentially could have rung when the receptionist breezily told me that the yoga class time had changed but there was something very similar on instead that was very popular. Apparently, I was in luck, because there was one space left and the bouncy, young receptionist was sure that I would love it. She swiftly swiped my membership card and I naively took the ticket she returned with the card, before heading to the loos for a last minute, precautionary, pre-exercise class wee. Let's face it after four babies one's pelvic floor isn't what it was, regardless of how conscientiously one does those exercises recommended by the health visitor all those years ago.

Having completed my visit to the ladies I came out of the swing door to experience a total assault on my visual senses. A figure encased almost entirely in luminous orange, green and yellow leopard print erupted from the gent's toilets at speed and almost mowed me down.

The Luminous Leopard flung his lower arms up from the elbow in horror, wrists flicked back as he trilled "Oops! Sorry!" ever so cheerfully. Turning sideways he shimmied past me flashing me the sweetest smile as he went. I smiled back, involuntarily, reeling just a bit with shock at the contrast his bright white teeth made with the deep fake tan of his skin.

'There goes a supremely confident individual,' I thought to myself as I watched him sashay off down the corridor in his tight leggings. Pulling myself together I shuffled off towards Studio One and what used to be yoga but was now something else.

I probably should have been concerned by the sheer number of people waiting outside the studio for the class, or the fact that they were all at least half my age and dressed (or rather more accurately, not very dressed at all) in teeny tiny bits of tight, bright Lycra, however I was tired and not really paying enough attention. Anyway, if this new class was similar to yoga then it couldn't be too bad, surely?

When the studio doors opened and the sorts of ladies I was expecting to attend a yoga class, all carrying yoga mats a bit like mine, poured *out* of the room and all the very young men and women that I was standing with poured in, I began to get cold feet. Nevertheless, the sheer volume of the crowd surging into the studio simply carried me along helplessly. Once inside, standing at the edge of the room in shock and clutching my yoga mat for dear life, I looked around in bemusement. What on earth was going on?

My luminous friend from the loos, in all his leopard print glory, sauntered up to me with one of those microphone headsets on, and patted me on the shoulder. "How lovely to see someone new today," he squealed delightedly. He grabbed my yoga mat and flung it to the side of the room. "You won't need that dear, have a couple of these instead." Thrusting two small plastic sticks from a bright blue, bucket he had hanging from one elbow, into my empty hands, he continued, "Now don't worry if you can't follow everything, just go with the flow. OK? Enjoy! You'll feel like a new woman after this."

Without waiting for a response he bounced off like an over excitable puppy, handing out plastic sticks to everyone else and after that bounded over to the door to the studio, closed it and *switched off the light!*

What?!?

I will admit that up until that point I had been considering quietly trying to sidle off towards the door and leaving unobtrusively, but I realised my chances of finding the door successfully were significantly reduced in the dark.

That was when the music started, really loud music with a heavy beat. I had no idea what band was playing, or even what genre of music it was other than *very modern*, but they were belting it out with impressive enthusiasm. Following that, a machine was turned on that sent a glitter-ball effect of tiny pinpricks of light dancing around the room.

Weirder and weirder!

I have to confess that I wasn't feeling terribly de-stressed right then.

The Luminous Leopard started to talk (ok, I really mean shout) over the music into his microphone headset "Right everybody, let's get moving and have some fun. Put your hands in the air!"

I noticed that suddenly there were a lot of bright lights being waved about in the air around me and realised that what I had been handed earlier was a pair of glow sticks. Fidgeting around at the bases of these I found a couple of switches and turned them on.

"Here we go!" Luminous Leopard started to talk the class through a series of complicated dance routines that I hadn't got a hope in hell of following, even if I could see what he was doing, but I did my best. Eventually I realised that if I couldn't actually see anyone else in the room apart from their glow sticks, then they probably couldn't see me either. So I concentrated on just making my glow sticks do what everyone else's glow sticks were doing whilst shuffling about from side to side. After a while I started to pick up some of the basic routine which, beneath all of the fancy flourishes, turns and kicks that the Leopard was banging on about through his microphone, was actually quite simple and very repetitive.

I have heard it said that you don't have to dance to the same tune as everyone else, and I certainly wasn't this evening. (Well, strictly speaking the tune was the same, but my dancing was definitely unique.)

I was surprised to find that this whole 'exercising in the dark' lark was really very liberating because I could just enjoy it without wondering if anyone could see my flabby bits wobbling around. In fact, in the dark no one can see you at all, let alone your flabby bits, so all I had to do was just chill and go with the flow as the Luminous Leopard had so wisely advised.

I am quite sure that I got everything wrong. After all I am very aware that I have little to no co-ordination, but I just didn't care. It was like being in a protected, little bubble, away from the rest of the world and all my worries. All I focussed on were the glow sticks and the beat of the music. (And not bumping into the person next to me in the dark of course!) By the end of the fifty-five minute class I was drenched in sweat but I found that I had really enjoyed myself.

Never in a million years would I have willingly chosen to go to a 'Clubercise' class (it is part of the scary, high intensity bit of the class timetable and therefore automatically on my 'do-not-do-list') but I was seriously considering doing it again. It was great fun!

I whizzed off home in an exhausted cloud of euphoria, leaving all the barely dressed young things in Lycra to trot off to the bar and flirt outrageously with each other. A short while later I skipped into the house past Beloved Husband and the Barbarians humming happily to myself.

"Do I take it that the yoga was a success?" asked Beloved Husband.

"In a way!" I said with a mysterious smile as I headed for the shower. There's no way I was telling him or the boys what I'd really been up to, they might die laughing and I wouldn't want that.

PART 3

On ne saurait faire d'omelette sans casser des œufs …

One cannot make an omelette without breaking eggs…

François de Charette.
1763 -1796

11: Deconstruction

Definition: to take apart

Back with the construction project in the past…

As with many things it is often a factor that things need to get worse before they can get better. In the case of the cottage it was necessary for a degree of demolition to take place before any useful construction could be achieved.

Interestingly, it would appear that someone had felt that Skelly would enjoy watching the rebuild project, as he had migrated from his position on the back patio and was now present on the driveway. Wearing a fluorescent yellow jacket, he was comfortably ensconced on my little bench, which had been relocated next to the side of the garage in order to facilitate a prime view of proceedings.

Fortunately the builders didn't bat an eyelid at their unusual audience and carried on regardless. They've probably seen it all before, although I am pretty certain most normal families keep their skeletons locked up in dark cupboards rather than openly flaunting them in the front garden for all to see; then again you probably know by now that we are not normal.

By 9.30am on the second day of the rebuild project, everyone had already had a very busy morning indeed.

After many fruitless phone calls on my part to the electricity company and also the telephone company, over the previous months, to ask them to come and make the mains electrics and telephone lines that were dangling precariously from the damage gable wall safe, I had given up. However it would appear that my builders had more influence than I, because all of a sudden two engineers, one from each of the electricity and telephone companies had arrived that morning at 8.30. Their brief was to remove the hazardous mains electrics cable and the telephone line from the top of the crumbling cob wall under the thatch, and reattach them to a section of more stable wall under the slate roof to the rear of the house.

After a bit of “you first”, “no, no, you first” to-ing and fro-ing from these two engineers, I finally solved their polite procrastination by firmly suggesting that the safest option for everyone was to sort out the mains electricity first, so that the telephone engineer couldn’t possibly be accidentally electrocuted as he moved the telephone line. Once that was established my nice builders peeled off the black plastic sheeting that had enshrined the cottage for so many months and the engineers got to work.

Shortly thereafter, ‘death by falling electricity cable’ had been removed from the morning’s agenda and the telephone line was also reattached to a more stable part of the house. The visiting engineers disappeared as suddenly as they had arrived and our builders could at last get on with taking down the damaged wall.

The plan for the next few weeks was to remove the crumbling gable wall first (leaving the damaged front wall) in situ, then digging a foundation trench and filling it with concrete. When the concrete was set, a new gable wall would be constructed over it, using cement block work with a cavity, in accordance with appropriate modern building methods. As soon as that reached roof height and had set, it would be able to take the weight of the roof; then the same process would be done for the damaged cob wall at the front of the house. Steel rods would be run through the two sets of foundations in order to bond them together and the block work of the two walls would be interlinked, retrospectively, for additional strength. The new walls would then be tied in to the remaining two undamaged cob walls using steel bars.

But that was for a later date, for now the first damaged wall had to be deconstructed.

The Boss had assured me that this would be done in a carefully controlled manner. However after watching this particular stage I was beginning to think that The Boss and his building team had very different definitions of both the word 'careful' and the word 'controlled'.

Five minutes after The Boss had left the property, the builders' radio was cranked up to full volume and Thor was dancing around on top of the thatched roof above the damaged gable. (How on earth had he got up there so quickly?) He was welly-ing the chimney rhythmically with his sledgehammer, whilst singing Queen's 'Bohemian Rhapsody' at the top of his voice. (My dear neighbours please forgive me.)

Occasionally he would get a bit distracted during his accompanying dance routine and start smacking the other chimney too.

When this happened, Lofty would quickly stand up from where he was putting together a scaffolding tower with Shy Guy and yell at him, "Wrong one, mate! That one is staying! And be careful!" Thor would pause, shrug and skip back along the ridge to the right chimney and resume his whacking with renewed enthusiasm.

From my perch next to Skelly on the bench by the garage, I began to suspect that Thor might have some ADHD issues.

Although the chimney stack over the damaged gable did put up a valiant fight, it eventually conceded to the demands of the sledgehammer. Then, once the weight of the stack was gone, it was time to start on the removal of the cob wall.

Never in my entire life had I thought I would ever willingly allow someone to take a pneumatic drill to the side of my house. Yet there I was, shivering in the January wind, watching in fascination as huge holes were repeatedly drilled into the side of my home.

You might ask why the drill was necessary after all if they just took the external suporting props away, surely it would just fall down, wouldn't it? That was rather the point though. The cob was already cracked and disintegrating but the wall needed to be brought down in a controlled manner so that no additional damage was done and nobody injured. Hopefully this meant a significantly more controlled manner than the chimney dismantling operation I had just witnessed.

Thus Lofty and Shy Guy, stood at the top of the newly erected scaffolding tower, were drilling into the damaged wall with grim determination. Beginning at the peak of the damaged gable wall they cut the cob into manageable sized chunks that could be lowered safely to the ground and put into a waiting skip. It was slow, heavy work and I found it surprisingly exhausting to watch.

Controlled and safe it might be but the amount of dust generated was unbelievable. It went everywhere.

It is a most surreal experience to watch from the outside while one of the rooms of your home is being revealed inch by inch from the ceiling down, as the side of your house is taken apart. Eventually I couldn't take it anymore and went back round to the back of the house, to put the kettle on and try to calm down.

After several hours I returned to the work site laden with refreshments for the builders. By then it was possible to see directly into the first floor of the house and what had formerly been Quiet's bedroom. You could still see his big, old wardrobe standing where the corner of the room used to be, the door wide open, as if he were up there, in the middle of choosing an outfit for the day.

It felt so wrong.

I became aware of a warm presence next to me and turned my head to see Quiet, standing beside me, his hands deep in his pockets, staring up into his old room with an unfathomable look on his face.

"You OK?" I asked.

He shrugged and sighed heavily all the while his gaze was locked on his former bedroom. Wondering what was going through his mind, I tucked my hand through his arm, squeezed it comfortingly and we just stood there watching for a while in silence before we retreated to the relative warmth of the back of the house.

Logic had got the fire going in the grate earlier on and it was doing its best to successfully counter the January chill. Deciding that comfort food was needed to cheer us all up and help keep us warm, I rummaged through the fridge for ingredients and set about making bangers and mash with peas and gravy for lunch.

It was the last day of the school Christmas holidays, so the afternoon was spent trying to encourage the Barbarians to check their school bags, finish any remaining homework as well as locating their clean uniform and sports kits so that the school run the next day could take place in an organised fashion. There was little hope of actually achieving any degree of true efficiency, considering the circumstance under which we were living, but I felt I had to try.

Later that afternoon I popped round to the front of the house to see what progress had been made. As the early darkness of winter was falling, work had to stop and the plastic sheets were being wrapped back around the cottage walls. Only now, almost the entire gable side of the house was missing. It looked as if someone had sliced into a Battenberg cake revealing the coloured layers inside. From the road and driveway you could see right into the side of our home on three storeys, the loft at the top, then the bedrooms upstairs, the remainder of the stairwell and study downstairs as well as all the layers of the damaged floors, ceilings and joists in between.

I could see lightshades dangling in the middle of the ceilings, carefully chosen wallpaper and much loved posters still adorning what was left of the internal walls. Random, abandoned bits of furniture that we hadn't been able to remove stood exactly where we had left them. It was our home but at the same time it wasn't.

How peculiar!

It was like looking at a memory that didn't quite fit with what we thought we remembered, or a previously treasured photograph that was now battered and faded with age.

If I stood on my tiptoes, I could even see the door of the sealed off bedroom where the little girl on the swing was waiting for me.

I was glad that it was all hidden again behind the black plastic by the time Beloved Husband came home. The missing wall was concealed and the cottage looked normal again. Well, as normal as a cottage wrapped in black plastic can look, I suppose. Only Quiet and I had seen our home so exposed, as all the other Barbarians had quite sensibly stayed inside in the warm all day. I figured that there was no need for anyone else in the family to feel so unsettled unless it was unavoidable.

As usual Quiet wasn't talking but I couldn't tell if this was his normal sort of 'teenage boy' not-talking or whether it was a new more sinister 'definitely upset' kind of not-talking. I resolved to keep a close eye on him as I rustled up supper that evening.

12: Practice

Definition: to perform an action repeatedly in order to acquire a degree of skill

Back to the present...

Surprisingly enough, I woke up the morning after my Clubercise class feeling pretty good in spite of several previously unknown (and now rather sore) muscles I must have identified with all that strenuous 'dancing'. I realised that I had slept right through the night with no nightmares disturbing me. Result!

Even the school run and a rather tedious morning at work didn't dent my enthusiasm for the day, so as soon as I made it home just after lunch I shot into my little studio and started to rummage around in my boxes of art supplies intending to start a new painting.

After my visit to the GP, I had finally finished my wobbly silver fish painting by following her advice to adapt my painting technique. By letting the thick paint dry I was then able to let my hand rest directly on the canvas to steady it while I marked in the final little fish. Just because this wasn't how I usually did things didn't mean it shouldn't be done. The result was remarkably successful and any inadvertent wobbling in the new layer of paint, I felt could be attributed to an attempt to create the illusion of movement in the water.

Buoyed up by this triumph I had started to look into other painting techniques and spent rather along time on YouTube researching new ideas and then experimenting. I particularly liked the concept of mixed media pieces and had started to adapt my ideas to incorporate the use of textured canvases and other layering and staged techniques. Some of these experiments worked and some didn't, either way it was exciting and really rather fun. Change really wasn't such a bad thing.

While I was digging into a large box of equipment that sits under my desk next to the easel, my fingers brushed against a bubble wrapped package, stuffed right at the back. I'd always known was there but had been studiously ignoring it. It was about the size of an A4 piece of paper and as thick as a pack of cards. I gently withdrew the package and turned it over in my hands thoughtfully.

My musings were interrupted by the noise of a Skype call on the IPad. Instantly my mothering instincts were on red alert. I had already spoken to the girls briefly that morning, and no one else skypes me, so why were they calling again? Placing the package on the windowsill next to the desk, where I could ignore it for a bit longer, I flicked the iPad on to accept a call from Logic.

"Are you OK?" I asked.

She frowned, "Yes, I'm fine. Calm down! You're supposed to be trying to be less stressed remember, not more. I just forgot to mention something earlier."

"Oh!" I relaxed, "What was that then?"

"I wanted to know how you were finding the whole decaf tea thing."

"Umm. Not so good actually." I confessed looking at the barely touched cup of decaf tea in front of me. "I don't really like it so it's a bit of a struggle. I am trying though. It's been three weeks now since I had a cup of the real stuff but I have to admit I really want one."

"Well there's this guy on my course who told me that there are still traces of caffeine in decaf tea and coffee," she said.

"Really?" I asked. "Are you sure?"

"Yeah. There's this other girl too, who agreed with him. She's a bit of a hippy type and lives down the hall from me. She's really into all that new-age stuff. Apparently she's trying to 'find' herself. I don't understand why though, she's eighteen! Surely she should have worked out who she is by now?" said Logic with the absolute confidence of one who has never had any doubt with regard to her own personal identity. "Anyway she said that you needed to be drinking herbal teas and stuff like that to be truly off caffeine."

"Ugh!"

"Yeah, I know! But she says that it's easier to do if you are completely caffeine free. I don't know if it's true or not, but it might be worth a try. Have you thought about hot water with fresh lemon juice in it? It's quite nice, especially if you add honey rather than sugar, then it's a bit healthier. Try it and let me know what you think. Anyway it was only a quick call to ask if you wanted me to see if that girl knows any really good herbal teas or coffee substitutes that she'd recommend. There might be one you actually like."

"I doubt it," I responded gloomily. "But, OK thanks."

"Sure, call you later then. Bye!" She was gone again. It was nice that she was trying to help me. I decided that I'd better make sure I stayed on the no-caffeine waggon and try to help myself too. Next step, perhaps a real yoga class or something similar tonight. Maybe with inner peace I would also find a liking for herbal teas especially if Logic's hippy friend could recommend some that didn't taste of cat's pee.

Smiling at the thought I reminded myself that shaky hands and a few nightmares weren't the end of the world. My heart was fine. The six of us were still a family, even though our girls had left home. This was just a different phase in our lives together. We had each other. We were going to be fine.

I turned to a small canvas board and started to work on a blue and white seascape scene reminiscent of the end of a long sunny day on a Cornish beach holiday, all sparkling water and silhouettes. Before long I had created the outline of a small boy running into the picture towards the sea and chasing seagulls to make them take off into the air. It was a very free and easy piece with not too much fine detail, so my tremor hadn't interfered particularly with what I was trying to achieve. The doctor was quite correct when she had said that there were ways of adapting my art to fit my abilities and I ought to put my mind to exploring more of that.

It did occur to me to wonder if an element of the shaky painting hands might also be down to lack of practice. In the past I had painted prolifically. Every day I had worked on finely detailed pieces. It was very true that I hadn't completed anything that required that sort of precision for a very long time, but I hadn't really wanted to. The pieces I worked on now were generally large, colourful energetic pieces that didn't need too much detail. They were pleasing to the eye, really fun to paint and helped me relax.

It could be argued that I should probably put in some fine brushwork practice and see if that bore any fruit. There was only one way to find out so I dug out a new blank sheet of canvas paper as well as a series of small brushes and set about putting my right hand muscles through a whole series of painting exercises that required precise movements and fine brush control. The results were total rubbish if I am completely honest, but no matter how disheartening this was, I resolved to do the exercises every day, without fail, to see if things improved.

After all, it has to be said that the only true failure in life is a failure to try.

***

The brush manipulation exercises were not as immediately successful as I had hoped they would be and this rather underlined just quite how bad my fine motor control had become. The tremor was still very pronounced which I found depressing. I thought I had hidden my feelings quite well, but it was brought to my attention later that week that I might have been rather grumpy, when the fellas in the family joined forced to try and persuade me to go out for the evening on my own.

Now there was a time many years ago, when Beloved Husband had been somewhat nervous about being left alone with the children given their rather uncivilised behaviour. (Hence their affectionate nick name 'The Barbarians'.)

I was reminded of one particular Saturday morning when Supreme-Parent-in-Charge duties fell to Beloved Husband. He was to escort Quiet to a party. All suggestions on my part that it would be prudent to keep our mild-mannered, four year old Barbarian away from a specific brand of small, round, highly coloured, chewy sweets were brushed aside. He could cope, he said confidently. Did I not trust him? I wisely invoked the Fifth Amendment at that point. In all fairness, I should point out that, although I had witnessed several occasions when our calm and contented, silent third child had achieved a transformation similar to that of Bruce Banner becoming The Hulk, following the consumption of that particular brand of sweets, my Beloved Husband had not.

Long story short: an hour later he was obliged to use super-human effort to contain the uncontainable, in order to extract Quiet from the party and return him home in one piece. Pulling onto the drive looking grey, sweaty and exhausted Beloved Husband uttered these immortal words: "You were right," before falling out of the car and dragging himself into the house. Under the circumstances I didn't feel that the words "I told you so" would be terribly well received, but that didn't stop me thinking them! I merely smiled and leaned into the back of the car to release the Incredible Hulk from his car seat, although, on reflection it might have been wiser to leave him there until Bruce Banner had reappeared!

Over the years the Barbarians had been civilised and now were fully equipped with all the necessary social graces to fit in with society. Hence Beloved Husband felt fully confident about making a concerted effort to get rid of me for the evening. No doubt this was because there was some sporting match on the telly that he and the boys wanted to slob-out in front of, eating junk food and yelling "Foul!" at regular intervals whilst exclaiming loudly at the referee. It appeared that the boys agreed with him that a grumpy wife and mother would just get in the way. (Obviously neither of them was particularly hungry at that point.)

Small sweetly suggested that I might like to go to another Yoga class, as I had seemed to enjoy the last one so much. Beloved Husband agreed that this might be a good plan and hinted that he would give me a lift, no doubt so that he could be sure that I went.

Quiet joined in at that point, peeling his eyes off his IPod and running them down the list of gym classes on the noticeboard on the wall next to him. "There's one of those Tai thingy classes you were on about the other day at 8 o'clock in Studio 3." He said encouragingly after a brief look, "It says it's for seniors so you'll fit right in!"

"Thank you very much!" I exclaimed "I'm not that old! I'll have you know that I am only in my mid-forties!" Cheeky beggar!

"I was only saying what it says here, but if you think it'll be too much for you, don't go." He shrugged and returned his attention to his social media account.

"It's not going to be too much for me!" I insisted adamantly.

“Fine, go then,” he said, as if it made no difference to him either way, which it probably didn’t.

“OK, I will,” I said.

“Great,” said Beloved Husband, relieved that a decision had been made. “Go get changed and I’ll drop you off. I can come back for you after the football is finished.”

Aha, so I was right, there was a match on and the boys wanted to get shot of the grumpy girl in the house.

The thought of a gentle Tai Chi class for senior citizens did sound rather relaxing. Not that I know anything about Tai Chi you understand. Or senior citizens either, for that matter, they could be a really energetic bunch. Either way it had to be a major improvement on listening to the boys shouting at the TV all evening.

13: Quandary

Definition: being in a state of perplexity over a troublesome decision between two or more equally undesirable alternatives

Back to the repair job in the past...

The first school run of the January term took place the next morning with no real disasters. Well! I say that, but I really mean no disasters that I didn't manage to solve.

I felt we did extremely well in our leaving-the-caravan-and-escaping-to-school-and-work routine. All Barbarians had got up, showered and dressed with minimal grumbling. Breakfast had happened and all necessary elements of educational paraphernalia were appropriated. So off we had set to the various schools in fairly good time.

Now ordinarily I would advocate that the older Barbarians should use the school bus, after all if there is a splendidly civilised service like that available in the country, then we should make use of it. Use it or lose it. (Plus it makes my life so much easier.)

Nevertheless they do have to walk quite a long way to get to the bus stop (a glorified term for the corner of a muddy field, a bit closer to civilisation than our house) as we do live in the middle of nowhere. Added to that minor inconvenience the bus always arrived at a disgustingly early hour in the morning as there were quite a few other remote hamlets for it to grace with its presence before it could return to the sophistication of the urban environment and the school gates.

I take my hat off to the brave bus driver who does venture out this far, as he has to stop at every little lay-by and cross roads on his tortuous route; after all if he's here with a bus, then he might as well fill it. However he does run the risk of getting stuck behind slow moving tractors and being forced to suddenly avoid any number of random livestock wandering across the road unexpectedly. This could include anything from ducks and chickens to wild ponies ambling into his path; to say nothing of cats, rats, or slinky wild ferrets moving at speed. Then there were the herds of cows, udders heavy with milk, ponderously crossing from the fields to the milking parlour at regular intervals.

Our gallant bus driver has also been known to rescue the odd motorist stuck in the water-logged ditches. These fiendish traps lurked in the undergrowth at the side of the road, ready to trap those impatient persons that attempted to squeeze past the slow moving bus on the narrow, single-track country lanes. These drivers had no idea they were taking their lives in their hands by driving on the overgrown verges rather than reversing back to the designated passing place and waiting to let the bus pass.

Amazingly this intrepid hero successfully drags his laden vehicle back to the metropolis and through the school gates by what feels to him like lunch time, even though it is usually only just past 8.45am, on a daily basis. As the students spill out of the bus to slope off to whichever classroom they need first, the driver staggers to the canteen where the catering supervisor keeps a vat of strong coffee waiting for him with a large sticky bun to settle his nerves. Then, at 3pm in the afternoon, he does the whole thing again in reverse. (The route is in reverse, obviously, not the bus!)

What a hero!

Anyway, brave bus drivers aside, Chaos and Logic were now in the midst of the build up to the A level and AS level exam period and, as the potential for drama and excitement on the aforementioned school bus added a certain amount of stress to the start of their day, I had taken to driving them into the sixth form to ensure they arrived in a relatively calm and collected condition.

As I triumphantly swung into a space outside the sixth form entrance and pulled on the handbrake there was a gasp of horror from Chaos who was sat beside me. My heart sank! What had we (she) forgotten?

Looking over at her I saw genuine alarm in her eyes.

OK! Bracing myself I raised my eyebrows at her questioningly and I watched her face crumple as she said "Mum! I'm still wearing my slippers!"

"Ah!"

Both boys dissolved into a heap of unhelpful hysterical laughter in the back of the car while Chaos and I both looked tentatively down into the passenger side foot well. True enough, there on her feet were a pair of pink, fluffy, bunny rabbit slippers complete with floppy ears and whiskers. Seriously, how had we all missed them as she got into the car earlier on?

To give me my due, while my initial reaction was that the slippers did have a good sturdy sole and would probably stand up quite well to a whole day walking around the sixth form college, I did accept that her social reputation would not survive in a similarly hardened condition.

There are times as a parent when we must make extreme sacrifices. The demand comes upon us when we least expect it and solutions can require the most painful of concessions.

With a heavy sigh I knew I was going to have to pay the ultimate forfeit.

Looking down at my brand new (size five) shiny, black ankle boots I gave them a sad, mental goodbye. I had worn them for less than an hour. Closing my eyes I slipped them off my feet and handed them over, wincing as she shoved her (size 6) feet into them gratefully.

"Mum! You are a star!" she said. "They're a bit tight but I'll be fine! Don't worry." she said with a relieved smile and a quick kiss of gratitude, before climbing out of the car. While I hadn't been remotely worried about her feet, I knew that my poor boots were never going to be quite the same again.

Quiet was still shaking with laughter as I watched the girls head off to their lessons.

"Are you going to get out then?" I prompted sharply. His secondary school was on the same campus as the sixth form so this was his stop too. Pulling himself together he opened the rear door and stepped out, then, still sniggering he stuck his head back in and said "You do realise you've got the primary school drop to do now, don't you?"

"Oh Heck!" he was right! Sighing heavily, I accepted that I was going to have to drop Small off in the school playground wearing pink bunny rabbit slippers. Funnily enough, Small immediately stopped laughing in the back of the car once the full potential horror of this particular outcome dawned on him.

After that, I was going to have to drive home and walk past the builders wearing the slippers in order to get to the caravan so that I could change into a proper pair of shoes and then go on to work. Late!

Great!

It turned out that my luck was in that morning as I was able to palm a very subdued Small off on another mother in the school carpark, without having to set foot outside my vehicle. Not surprisingly this was a solution that my youngest was more than happy to co-operate with, thank goodness! Phew! One problem at a time!

Arriving back at the house I squared my shoulders and decided to simply brazen it out, walking with a confidence I didn't feel across the drive towards the caravan braced for any comments. But the building team were too busy playing with Skelly to notice me.

On my return from the caravan, with suitable work shoes appropriated, I noted that Skelly now sported a fetching blue hard hat, a packet of Marlboro Lights stuffed into the top pocket of a fluorescent yellow jacket and a copy of The Sun tucked under one arm. I gave the boys a grin of approval for their handy work and set off to work where a nice, warm, dust free office full of left over Christmas biscuits and cake awaited me.

****

When I returned from work later that afternoon, it was obvious that the work on the gable wall had cracked on a pace. No sooner than the cob was down then the lads had started digging the foundation trench.

That evening the Boss kept me fully informed of what was going on, when and why, which was fascinating, but in some ways it might have been easier not to know. I told you I was contrary. Only a few chapters back I was grumbling about not being told anything and now I am doing the same because I have too much information. It just gives me more to worry about.

Too much information is the reason I spent three whole nights in a row watching the thermometer readings of the external air temperature. The Boss had explained that laying foundation concrete in cold weather wasn't ideal (I've had enough of 'not ideal' now, I want ideal!), but that as long as the temperature didn't drop below freezing all would be well. Just for a change!

Fortunately there are all sorts of precautions you can take to make sure your concrete sets beautifully in colder temperatures and The Boss' team had implemented them all so no problems were anticipated. Nevertheless I latched on to the fact that it was January and pretty damn cold. Adding in my overall bad luck factor I was convinced that it would freeze and the concrete would be ruined, hence my nocturnal obsession with the outside temperature. Noticing my concern, Chaos kindly gave me a lengthy lecture on the amount of heat produced by the chemical reaction that takes place in setting concrete, and explained that this would off-set the dropping external temperatures. Eventually I simply had to accept that it was all way beyond me and so tried to make myself relax.

As luck would have it, we experienced a very mild two week period just at the critical concrete setting stage so my fears were unfounded. The new concrete block wall grew quickly upwards to meet the roof and as soon as that was strong, the builders turned their attention to demolishing the second wall. All seemed to be going to plan and I started to think that everything was going to be ok.

Silly me!

That, of course, was a big mistake!

Huge!

Soon after the second wall started to come down, the Boss and Genuine Old Building Expert came around to the back of the house to have a little chat with Beloved Husband and I. We all sat around the table in the conservatory with hot cups of tea and the plans for the rebuild were spread out so that they could update us on the progress of the work.

This was the point at which Beloved Husband asked the question that had been bothering us both for quite a while.

“How effective is the repair plan when it comes to tying the new walls into the remaining cob walls?”

The Boss and Genuine Old Building Expert exchanged a long speaking look.

We probably should have kept quiet and jollied on through life oblivious to reality, but we didn't. Having asked the question we were going to have to deal with the answer which was basically: not very effective.

The insurance company had been understandably intent on restricting their own liability on this job. As a result, we now had a repair plan which, while fit for purpose in the short term, had some serious potential flaws when it came to long term sustainability.

Genuine Old Building Expert agreed that it was definitely possible to tie the old and new walls together effectively but that with the dissimilar material types expanding and contracting differently with temperature changes, over time there would always be likely to be a 'crack' of some sorts at the juncture. While this crack would not necessarily be a structural problem it would definitely be a cosmetic one and would influence the value and potential saleability of the property.

The second issue with the plan on the table was that it left two cob walls in situ. This was potentially a big problem. Cob works most effectively as a single, solid, ring-like (or a square with rounded corners) structure. If you remove half of this then what is left is always going to fail eventually.

The insurance company were not going to replace the two walls left because they weren't failing yet. The key word in that sentence was 'yet'. The two remaining cob walls represented a ticking time bomb that would definitely fail at some point in the future.

The Boss and Genuine Old Building Expert reassured us that this was likely to be quite some time in the future and that the repair as designed on the plans before us would work in the short term, but they couldn't guarantee that we wouldn't have major problems in the future.

In short what really needed to be done, to prevent our being put back in this position again, was to take out all four cob walls and rebuild the whole cob section of the house.

Thus, to paraphrase the immortal words of Jane Austin 'an unhappy alternative was before us'. We could allow the repair to progress as the insurance company had devised it and risk putting our children through their home collapsing again in the future. We could of course attempt to sell the repaired building, but we didn't fancy our chances of being able to do that, especially as any structural survey would identify the potential risk and make it impossible to sell anyway. Who would take it on?

The alternative was to extend the repair job to include the removal of the other two cob walls and to find the money to pay for it ourselves. We were already going to have to find extra finances to cover the installation of a concrete floor to meet building regulations on the repair. In addition to this there were going to have to be significant repairs to the central ground floor ceiling/first storey floor joists and boarding as well as the same for the loft.

A new staircase was required too, as the insurance company repair plan didn't have any contingency built into it for that aspect of the job either. Then there would be costs associated with redecorating throughout and carpeting or flooring. Apparently all of those would count as material gain and we weren't allowed that unless we paid for it ourselves.

There was some good news though, when the first gable wall came down, Genuine Old Building Expert had been able to confirm that the back section of the house had been built entirely independently of the cob at the front. Apparently it had been built as close to the cob wall as possible, with a gap of a few centimetres which had then been stuffed with straw and sealed over with render. This meant that the whole of the kitchen/lounge/conservatory was completely stable and unaffected by the damage at the front. Isn't hindsight a wonderful thing? It would have helped us enormously to have known that last year! Anyway, as a result of this information we could be confident that removing the entirety of the cob would not cause any structural issues with the back of the property. Thank heaven for small mercies!

The Boss and Genuine Old Building Expert left us to think through our options. It was obviously not a fun part of their job, but it was important that they gave us a full and honest picture of the potential pitfalls of the repair in progress. Now we just had to decide on our next move.

The obvious choice was to remove all of the cob walls and do a proper complete repair job rather than the more short term solution that the insurance company was proposing. The problem was that our finances were stretched really tight and we were looking at having to find a not insignificant amount of money for the full repair.

Beloved Husband and I sat side by side at the table for a long time after they had left, each trying to mentally work through the implications of this new information with very heavy hearts. We felt we had come so close to fixing things only to have it all snatched away again. As I blinked rapidly trying to disperse the hot salty tears threatening to break free, I felt his hand reach for mine under the table and hold on tight.

"It'll be OK!" He murmured, "We'll sort it out."

14: Indomitable Spirit

Definition: an unconquerable warrior, a courage or will that cannot be overcome.

Returning to the present day and the new exercise schedule...

So half an hour after it was decided by the boys that I would attend a Tai Chi class, I found myself hastily dumped outside the leisure centre. After watching the three of them speeding off back to watch the football, I turned and hurried in the direction of Studio 3.

With only moments to spare before the class started, I bumbled through the studio door and put my bag down by the side of the room before turning around. I was a bit surprised by what I saw. This was not a room full of zen-like persons of a more mature generation, instead there were at least a dozen well-put-together gentlemen in their mid-thirties and forties all wearing loose white pyjama type outfits and looking at me with interest.

One of these fit-looking men (I mean sporty-looking 'fit' not the other type of 'fit', although now I come to think of it that alternative meaning applies too) came towards me.

"Welcome!" he said, smiling at me, "we always like to see new people in class. Have you done any Taekwondo before?"

What?

Taekwondo?

Looking at the other chaps in the room I noticed that they are all now tying impressive looking black belts with lots of gold embroidery around their white pyjama suits.

"No I haven't," I replied. "But I think I might have come to the wrong class. Perhaps I should come back another time?"

I started thinking about whether I could subtly edge towards the door.

"Well you would probably be better off in the junior belt class with the other beginners next time, rather than this senior class," he agreed, still smiling. "That's at 7 o'clock, but you are here now, so why not give it a go? Just take it easy and enjoy."

So, senior belts not senior citizens and Taekwondo not Tai Chi. Quiet had a lot to answer for. From now on I was going to be checking that class schedule very carefully indeed. Fool me once etc....

The instructor seemed so enthusiastic that it was impossible to grab my bag, sidle out and run for the hills. Promising myself that I could kill Quiet slowly later on if I survived, I returned his smile and said "Sure, why not?"

Addressing the whole room he called, "Line up everyone."

All of the black belted gents lined up in rows facing the instructor. Two of them gestured for me to join them in a row at the back.

"Copy us!" one said.

"Yeah! We'll show you what to do," said the other.

I smiled gratefully and shuffled into place between them as the class came to attention, bowed and started a series of warm up exercises.

I had expected to be massively out of my depth and to these expert taekwondo students I probably was. Nevertheless I was surprised to realise I was really enjoying myself. The warm up consisted of mainly exercises that I had done before, push-ups, sit-ups, squats, jogging on the spot, stretching etc. Given the fact that I had been attending random exercise classes two or three times a week for at least four months now, my fitness had obviously improved massively. I found that, with some encouragement from my two back row buddies, I could just about keep up, which gave me a bit of a buzz.

Then the class moved onto kicking drills and punch combinations moving forwards and backwards in formation in the rows that we had started in. The instructions were first given in Korean and then thankfully translated and demonstrated for me by the instructor.

Eventually we took a break for some water and the guys all started to put on protective equipment and pair up. Apparently the next bit of the class was for sparing (i.e. fighting matches).

Probably the largest bloke in the class came over to me and said, "We'll go together, OK?" He was huge! Made even more immense by the massive trunk protector, helmet, groin, shin and arm guards he was wearing. I wasn't going to argue with him.

"OK!" I swallowed nervously aware that I didn't have any protective equipment and mentally renewed my vow to make Quiet pay later.

If there ever was a later, of course!

I needn't have worried though. While the rest of the class spent the next half an hour happily kicking the stuffing out of each other, my large partner patiently taught me how to kick him. He never once kicked me back.

It is a novel experience kicking a big fella who simply smiles at you, says you need to kick him harder and then shows you how to improve your technique so that you can attack him more effectively. Not surprisingly, I found it exceedingly therapeutic and by the end of the class I was able to thank my partner, my back row buddies and the instructor with genuine enthusiasm.

As I made my way down the steps of the leisure centre after the class, looking for Beloved Husband my phone buzzed. A text message informed me that the football had gone into extra time so he was going to be a bit late picking me up. There was no point hanging around in the car park so I turned on my heel and went back into the building to head for the bar. Replying to his text I said I would get a glass of lemonade and read my kindle and that he should come in to the leisure centre and find me when he was ready.

On entering the bar I spotted the entire taekwondo class ordering a round of beers. It is very thirsty work kicking each other after all!

I am not quite sure what Beloved Husband thought when he arrived an hour later to find me sinking my second pint surrounded by my new martial arts mates. In my defence I was actually following the doctor's orders to the letter. She told me not to drink wine before bed, to do some exercise and to get out and socialise. Well! There I was doing all three.

***

The next morning after probably the best night's sleep I had had in over three years, I woke up feeling unusually cheerful. Admittedly I did have a slightly muzzy head, (two pints of lager will do that!) I also had a lot of very sore muscles, but that didn't stop me from feeling great. Obviously kicking people was good for me! I was going to have to make a point of doing it again.

After dropping the boys to school, I trotted off to work quite happily and as soon as my shift was over I whizzed around the supermarket to restock the kitchen cupboards for the Barbarians to forage through when they got home.

Once home, I took the opportunity to return my lovely neighbour's (now empty) vegetable basket, as I had spotted her car in her driveway. Whilst I was there she repeated an earlier invitation for me to join her as a guest for at an up-coming Women's Institute event in the village. Given my positive mood, following my brilliant night's sleep, I found myself agreeing to go along. The exercise classes were certainly proving to be fun so perhaps the Doctor's suggestion of some female company wasn't such a bad idea either, and if there's one place you can guarantee to find female company it's at the WI.

Feeling like I had made a massive step forward in my campaign to look after myself I trotted off home and made myself a large cup of hot water with lemon juice before settling down to more brush control exercises in my little studio with a renewed enthusiasm. I was determined to beat this anxiety issue. I was going to relax, get fit and stop being so grumpy. My hands were going to stop shaking. Positive thinking!

Everything was going to be OK!

After putting my brush technique through the full exercise programme I had devised for myself, I decided to do a little mixed media experiment on a small canvas in order to test my progress. Having prepared a textured canvas the previous day using crumpled up tissue paper and PVA glue, I selected a series of bright blue, green and silver acrylic paints and soon a light, tropical ocean unfolded before me with a bright, sparkling shoal of fish spiralling through it. Tiny iridescent scales decorated the larger fish, each one created using trimmed sequins which were glued directly into the wet paint adding to the textural dimension of the piece. It was careful, fiddly work and took ages. My hands still shook, but not to the extent that I couldn't function, so it was with some triumph that I sat back several hours later and looked at the finished piece before me.

I was so please with it that I didn't even mind when Quiet loomed behind me later that evening after supper and stood looking at it critically for some time.

"Hmmm!" he said in a very non-committal way. "More fish!"

"Yes," I agreed seriously, "But these are different fish. These are sparkly fish."

"Yeah," he said sounding very unimpressed. "It's all a bit glitter and unicorns, though isn't it? I didn't think that was your sort of thing."

I looked back at my painting and tilted my head on one side, "I suppose it is a bit glittery but I don't see any unicorns. Anyway, who says it's not my sort of thing? I quite like it. I plan to do some bigger ones."

"Oh great!" he said with typical teenage disgust, "You'll be painting rainbows next."

"Oh don't worry," I said reassuringly, "it probably won't ever get to that stage!" Crossing my fingers out of his line of sight, I surreptitiously nudged an extremely colourful canvas (depicting a patchwork toy teddy bear, each patch a different colour of the rainbow) with my foot, sliding it further behind the stack of large fish paintings leaning against the wall.

Small came into the studio then and stood behind his brother holding an apple in one hand. Torn between wanting to marvel at the fact that he was voluntarily eating fruit without being blackmailed into it, whilst not actually wanting to bring attention to it, I just smiled at him and said, "What do you think of my fish?"

"Cool," he said sparing the painting a brief glance before he leaned back against the wall, drew two more apples out of his pockets and started juggling with them. "So, how did you get it to sparkle like that then?" He was totally focused on the flight path of his apples as he spoke and failed to register my disappointment that he probably wasn't planning to eat them.

I should probably explain the apple juggling. The day before, following an incident with both boys, two tennis balls, a football and a large glass vase, Beloved Husband had banned all balls from the house. Employing the obtuse ingenuity of the young male mind, Small had started to use the contents of the fruit bowl as ball substitutes.

At least he seemed to like my painting.

Quiet leaned over and snatched one of the apples out of the air mid-juggle and said, "Like you know anything about art, shorty!" before running off. Small gave a loud yell and barrelled after him. I didn't give much for Quiet's chances if his brother caught up with him. He looked like he meant business and, as I have said before; he wasn't actually that small anymore.

I sighed heavily. Thank goodness I had agreed to go out this evening to that WI event. Female company was definitely in order. Even though I hated the idea of going into a room full of strangers on my own, I was going to be brave. I was a grown up after all!

Wasn't I?

***

Several hours later I was forced to re-evaluate just how grown up I actually was, when I found myself standing nervously outside the main door into the village hall. The WI meeting was to be held inside. My lovely neighbour had been obliged to go up early to help set up, so we hadn't travelled together, and I was now lingering in the car park trying to pluck up the courage to open the door and go in on my own.

Just as I was deciding that perhaps I would simply go home instead, a group of ladies arrived, all chattering and laughing as they made their way towards me. One of them smiled brightly at me and said "Hello, are you joining us tonight?"

I shuffled my feet shyly and nodded, trying to smile back and not really doing a very good job.

"Don't be nervous, we don't bite. I promise! Come on in." She opened the door and I found myself whisked into the warm noisy room along with the rest of their party. Before long my name had been ticked off on a list, I had located my lovely neighbour and we were all sat down together for the rest of the meeting.

All I can say is that it wasn't at all what I had expected a WI meeting to be. There was a lot of laughter that evening, the nice sort of laughter. Everyone I met was incredibly friendly and welcoming and I wasn't once made to feel inadequate because I don't make my own jam or knit my own socks! In fact, I enjoyed myself so much that by the end of the evening I was considering joining.

It would seem that the good doctor had been right once again!

PART 4

"Heaven knows we need never be ashamed of our tears,"

Charles Dickens, 1812 – 1870
(Great Expectations 1860)

15: Integrity

Definition: being of sound morals, having ethical principles

Back with the decision to be made about the wobbly walls in the past...

The next day was a Saturday and we had no plans at all. Ordinarily we would have liked a nice long lie in, but given the cramped conditions in the caravan, the icy cold temperatures and the sprightly starlings skipping around on the metal roof from half-past-extremely-early (whilst wearing their best hob-nailed boots) that wasn't really an option.

As it was, Beloved Husband and I had passed a disturbed night anyway, as we both tried to get our heads around the advice we had received from The Boss and Genuine Structural Engineer Man the previous day. Under the circumstances any hopes for a visit from the Sand Man were futile and we spent the hours tossing and turning from side to side repeatedly, much to the disgust of the other caravan occupants who objected to the distinct rocking motion this set off in the whole unit. We were both trying to mentally sort through the dilemma before us, but even as the sun started to come up we each individually found ourselves no closer to a conclusion.

We had spent rather a long part of the evening before discussing our options on the telephone with various members of our extended family. After all, one of the main benefits of being part of such a large clan, is that you can ring your parents or siblings up with really dim questions from time to time. Luckily my brother had had some experience of working in the building trade as a student, and while he didn't have any direct knowledge of cob buildings or their associated structural engineering issues, he knew a few people who did. After making several phone calls on our behalf, he eventually came back to us and confirmed that the advice that Genuine Old Building Expert and The Boss were giving us was legitimate. The best option in structural engineering terms for the long-term future of the house was to remove the cob entirely.

So at seven o'clock the following morning Beloved Husband and I gave up pretending to sleep and opted to go for a long walk instead. There would be no builders on site today. We had until Monday to make a decision. After pulling on multiple layers of thick fleece, with hats, gloves and walking boots, we opened the caravan door and stepped out into a crisp, white, beautifully frosty morning leaving the grumbling Barbarians to snuggle down under their duvets and go back to sleep.

Startled by the caravan door closing behind us, a Buzzard took off from his perch in one of the oak trees at the bottom of the garden. We watched as he then swooped almost noiselessly towards us across the lawn, his large wingspan a majestic collection of brown and white feathers creating a magnificent display against the frost-bound land. As he settled on a nearby fencepost with a noisy fluttering of wings, a single perfect feather floated to the ground by my feet. Bending down I picked it up examining its natural beauty close up.

Crunching my way across the frozen grass to the house, I carried the feather in to the kitchen and placed it on a shelf above the sink. Then Beloved Husband and I each grabbed a couple of bread rolls, stuffed them with left over sausages from the night before and headed off into the forest for a stomp.

Eventually, having munched our snacks in thoughtful silence, we started to chat through our various options again, but it wasn't until we reached the trig point out on the heathland to the north of our home that we finally came to a decision.

"I don't see that we can risk staying in that house if we only repair the two damaged walls. If there's any chance the remaining cob will fail at some point and the kids will be made homeless again......" I trailed off.

"The fundamental problem," Beloved Husband mused, "is that I don't think it would be fair to carry on with just this repair job and then sell a house with a significant potential problem on to another family."

"No!" I agreed. "That wouldn't be fair."

"We don't really have a lot of choice. We're going to have to take the structural engineer's advice and do the full 'cob-removal' option. It's the only thing to do! I don't see another way round this."

"But we can't afford it!"

"I know," he sighed. "The insurance company won't cover the cost of replacing the undamaged walls, as they are actually stable at the moment so not technically in need of repair."

"Meaning that we will have to find the money for it somehow," I said gloomily.

"It is the right thing to do. The good news is that the rest of the property is absolutely fine and won't be affected. Now that we know the cob was built entirely separately we can be certain that the disintegration at the front hasn't caused any damage to the back sections. So at least we know the absolute limits of this particular job. I suggest we crack on and get it done properly. Then we have options. There is a little wriggle room to extend the mortgage a bit which will cover part of the cost of the work. But after that we'll have to juggle things. It'll be a while before the bills start to come in. You never know what will happen; we might manage to hold on to the house, but then again maybe not."

"I could take on some extra shifts at work." I offered.

"That will help, but either way we have to accept that we will probably be forced to sell the house after the work is completed. I don't see how we can sustain a mortgage of that size for too long."

We were standing next to the trig point by then, a single concrete marker set at the highest bit of the common. I turned and stared out over the beautiful view of grey/white heathland rolling away from us down the hill towards the ancient woodland that we had just hiked through.

I didn't dare face Beloved Husband, because I was ashamed of the tears that were welling up in my eyes. Whilst I was frustrated with myself for being such a watering pot, I simply couldn't cope with the thought that my poor babies were going to lose their home anyway in spite of the brave way in which they had coped with everything so far. The Barbarians had been amazing, pulling together as a team over the last nine months. They had put up an incredible fight in order to not be split up and sent away last summer in the wake of the house collapsing. How on earth were we going to be able to tell them that we'd eventually lose their home anyway?

I genuinely felt that my heart might break. I couldn't believe that we were back here yet again. When the insurance company had finally agreed that we had a legitimate claim I had foolishly thought that our troubles were over. Yet it seemed that the fates had other ideas and we were to be play things for a bit longer. I could only hope that I had the strength to survive it.

Thousands of possible consequences crowded into my head all at once. What if, after spending so much of their later teen years living in such cold and miserable conditions in the garden with two stressed out and grumpy parents, our two girls went to university and decided never to come home again? It was a bit of a leap I know but I was afraid that they would leave and never want to come back. If we sold their childhood home then they wouldn't have any emotional ties to any new place we bought. We'd have no shared history there.

Beloved Husband wrapped his arms around me from behind and I leaned back into him and sighed. Everything was still and silent. The only movement came from the frosty clouds of our mingled breath in the air and the hot tears that spilled unchecked down my cheeks.

“I can tell you are fast forwarding to total disaster in your mind,” he murmured quietly. “You do have a tendency to jump to the worst possible outcome these days.”

“Hmm!” it was all I could manage around the lump in my throat.

“Whatever it is that you are frightened of probably won’t happen you know. Selling the house won’t be the end of the world. Let’s just take it one day at a time, OK?”

“It’s the right thing to do!” he continued quietly after a pause. “Let’s fix this house properly. It’s the only way to move this situation forward.”

We stood there in contemplative silence for several minutes before I could collect myself and answer him without my voice wobbling. “I know. You’re right.” I said “I am just so tired.”

Then Beloved Husband straightened up and squared his shoulders. “OK! Decision made!” he said firmly. “Let’s not tell the children yet,” he continued after a moment. “There’s no need to upset them unnecessarily. Who knows, we might find a way to keep the house, but if we don’t, we can be happy in another one. As long as we are all together, nothing else matters.”

He was right, of course, but it didn’t really make me feel any better about it. Grabbing my hand he gave it a little reassuring tug and we started back towards the house feeling the lighter for having decided how to handle things.

16: Jamboree

Definition: a large gathering, or a noisy boisterous celebration.

Back in the present...

The following weekend was a busy one. Due to the significant distances involved, not to mention the cost and basic travel times courtesy of British Rail's little foibles, visits home from university during term time were a rarity. However this weekend Chaos and Logic had both managed to plan a trip home to coincide with each other, so I was in anticipatory heaven. I couldn't wait to get all my chickens back under one roof, even though it would only be for two days. Their train journeys even overlapped for the final connection to the nearby town, which meant I could pick them both up from the local station at the same time, which was useful.

I had been looking forward to the six of us being back together again so very much, but I have to confess that I hadn't calculated on quite how much dirty washing would be descending on the house at the same time, as both girls staggered off the train with a hefty rucksack and a wheeled suitcase each, stuffed to bursting point with rancid raiment.

Fortunately, I reasoned that they had both become fairly self-sufficient as students and were quite capable of feeding the washing machine themselves, in between cups of tea and gossiping nineteen to the dozen. It wasn't long before the kitchen was full of happy chattering and bursts of loud laughter as the girls sorted through their light and dark loads. They were so grateful not to be stuck in some university launderette unable to leave the machine in case the cycle ended early and some other student emptied their clean washing onto the floor.

Knowing my daughters as I do, and hopeful that they might fill the freezer with some goodies for me, I had made sure to stock up on a good selection of potential savoury and sweet baking ingredients. So it wasn't long before normal service had been resumed. The oven and radio were switched on almost immediately we arrived home from the station and soon the aroma of fresh pasties, sausage rolls, sticky cakes and fresh cookies filled the air.

I watched Quiet with interest as he chatted casually away to Chaos, whilst carefully positioning himself in the most likely location to be able to snaffle hot sausage rolls as she unloaded the first trays from the oven. Small had cunningly persuaded Logic to let him help roll out the cookie mixture, so that he could take sneaky tasters of the raw dough when she wasn't looking. I think the boys had missed their sisters, although they wouldn't ever admit it of course.

Logic had brought home some organic maple syrup from the helpful hippy's highly-recommended health food shop and was working on some alternative recipes that had a lower refined sugar content. Chaos had come supplied with a special type of cleansing green tea that she had researched for me on the internet.

It was lovely to hear my four Barbarians chatting away to each other, teasing and laughing and keen to share their news, so as soon as I was supplied with an acceptably non-stimulating hot drink and some fresh maple, oat and cranberry (surprisingly tasty) cookies, I snuck off to do some painting, content to have my Barbarians all home again. The house felt right. It was full, even if it was only for a couple of days, so I was happy.

In that moment it occurred to me that the nourishment supplied from home baking is not so much to do with the end product, but with the process itself. The rich aromas of butter, flour and savoury or sweet mixes warming the air during their transformation from base ingredients to enchanting delicacy, speak so much of love and care, that they create an indefinable feeling of security and companionship. It's about family, friends and sharing, which is something you don't get to quite the same degree from shop bought equivalents. One home made short bread is infinitely more fulfilling than anything you can buy off the shelf, because it is part of something so much more significant.

I began to realise why all those shop bought treats had not been able to fill the huge void inside of me. It was as if I had been trying to fill in a deep, dark well of emptiness using tiny pebbles, so no wonder I had eaten entire packets with no discernible results. It wasn't actually the sugar I was craving it was the whole magical phenomenon of sharing, caring and belonging.

***

It doesn't take much to have a bit of an impromptu party when you are part of a big family. Just getting together creates a crowd. Listening to the noise of music and happy chitchat filtering into my studio from the kitchen I knew we were all going to have a fantastic weekend together.

I hauled out the colourful rainbow canvas I had hidden from Quiet previously and checked it over. It was one of a whole series of rainbow related paintings, the detail and complexity of which had increased significantly with each piece as my dexterity improved. It wouldn't take much to finish this one off. I smiled to myself, I knew he was only teasing me when he grumbled, but if he really didn't approve of rainbows he definitely wouldn't be very impressed with the series of paintings I was planning to do next. I had every intention of using glitter, unicorns and everything else besides. It was time to have some fun!

For some reason I had spent the last few weeks obsessed with images of feathers. In fact everywhere I turned it seemed a feather would appear. I had quite a collection of them now on windowsills and various shelves around the house. While I frequently find myself uncertain over the concept of the existence of a higher being I do sometimes wonder about guardian angels.

It struck me that our traumatic home collapse ordeal could be looked at two ways. Obviously, on the surface of things it was tragic and very upsetting, but I felt it was important to remember that a great deal of good had happened too. Those positive elements led me to suspect that someone had definitely been watching over us during that awful time that we lived in the garden, not knowing how we would manage to stay together and fix our home.

For example, that first day when the cottage walls actually gave way out of the blue, several massively important things should be remembered. Firstly there was no one inside the house to be hurt or killed by flying debris and falling masonry. Had the walls fallen at 2am not 2pm, then there is no doubt that we would all have been killed. But they didn't and we weren't! Secondly builders had appeared, completely unexpectedly, to pick up some equipment that they had left behind months before. They had been able to start attempting to stabilise the disintegrating structure almost immediately and the damage to the cottage was prevented from being so very much worse.

Then weeks later, just as Beloved Husband and I were facing the fact that we would have to split up the children and send them away indefinitely, the house insurance company agreed to supply us with a caravan so we could stay together.

In the years that have followed all the issues arising from the rebuild have each been solved one by one, to the point that the house is now absolutely perfect. The sole remaining issue, the overwhelming debt arising from the work, would eventually be solved with the sale of the house.

In that vein, the personal health issues I had been experiencing could be overcome too. I was very lucky that it wasn't anything more serious and was already making good progress. With the help and support of the rest of the family I had every confidence that we would beat this difficulty too. None of us could expect not to be affected by what had happened but we could take every step available to help ourselves to recover, thus limiting the hold that past events could have over us.

I was beginning to see that this was merely the next stage in our journey; just one step in a whole series of steps that we were taking in order to climb back up from rock bottom. It was definitely time to move forward. We would be fine. So I reached for a fresh canvas and whether Quiet approved or not I was planning a painting with my feathers as a tribute to our Guardian Angel whoever and wherever he or she might be.

***

A couple of hours later Chaos came into the studio.

"Wow!" she said. "Quiet said you were painting what he called 'fluffy stuff' but I didn't realise he meant actual feathers, but they look really good. Simple but powerful! Kind of spiritual!"

I looked at her closely to check she wasn't taking the mickey out of her old mum but realised that she was serious.

"Anyway, Logic wants you in the kitchen to try a new sort of cake out. She says the sugar content is quite low, but between you and me I can't tell the difference."

"Oh OK!" I said, "I need to clean these brushes off anyway." I may have sounded less than keen, but it was all a front because, of course, I was more than happy to try any sort of cake on any sort of occasion, low sugar or not. I headed for the kitchen but realised I had forgotten to bring my palette knife with me to wash too. Turning back into the studio I caught Chaos taking a photo of my feather painting on her phone.

She stopped when she saw me and looked guilty.

"What are you doing?" I asked curiously.

"Sorry, I should have asked first. Do you mind if I take a photo? I really like it." She said.

"No of course I don't, take as many as you like." I grabbed my knife and headed in the direction of the cake, assuming that she would follow me but she stayed in the studio quite a while before re-joining us.

***

A little later that evening we had all enjoyed a proper family supper, one that involved all six chairs around the expanded dining table for once. There was a great deal of joking around and teasing banter. I had cooked everyone's favourite, lasagne with salad and garlic bread. We rounded off the meal by each having a generous slice from a freshly baked, lemon drizzle cake that sat on a large plate in the middle of the table surrounded by big, fat, juicy strawberries.

Eventually, as Small was working his way through his second slice of cake, Chaos looked at Logic and raised a questioning eyebrow. Logic nodded. Turning towards Beloved Husband and me, Chaos shoved her empty cake plate aside, folded her arms on the table and leaned towards us saying, "We noticed the 'for sale' sign outside."

Beloved Husband and I exchanged a look and he said, "Yes, it is rather obvious isn't it? It's been up a couple of weeks."

"Yeah, we know," said Logic. "Quiet sent us a photo the day it went up. So what's going on?"

The reason for this joint visit home suddenly became clear. Other than getting their washing done, I mean. It seemed that the Barbarians were staging some sort of intervention.

OK! This should be interesting....

Small surreptitiously helped himself to a third slice of lemon cake elbowing his brother sharply for no reason whatsoever while he did it. Quiet grinned briefly and shoved him back hard, before looking down at his IPod and behaving as if he was totally deaf or on a different planet or possibly both. Beloved Husband reached over and neatly plucked the IPod out of Quiet's hand, putting it face down on the table in front of him.

"We did explain to both your brothers why we were going to put the house on the market, and we were planning on telling you as soon as you came back." As I listened to Beloved Husband speak, I kept my eyes down and examined the paint stains on my sleeve closely. I didn't feel I could look at the girls. I was really worried how they were going to take the news.

"Well! Here we are!" Chaos continued. "So tell us what's going on!"

"Well, your mother and I always knew that there was a risk we might have to sell the house after the rebuild was complete, because of the escalating costs that weren't covered by the house insurance policy. We didn't tell you because we were hoping that it might not be necessary. We've managed so far, and we could technically keep going if we have to, but it would take the pressure off us massively if we could sell up and move to something a bit more economical. So we thought we would put the place on the market and see what happened."

"That makes a lot of sense," said Logic. "It is an absolutely beautiful house now the work is all finished. We should get a really good price for it."

"I can't see there being any trouble getting a buyer," agreed Chaos. "Selling's a really good idea. Would it mean you could both take a bit of time off?"

"What do you mean?" asked Beloved Husband.

"She means we know that you are always working so hard trying to pay off the additional mortgage. If we sell the house and move somewhere more economical, will you both be able to work a bit less? So that we can see more of you?" asked Logic bluntly.

I looked up hopefully at the liberal sprinkling of the word 'we' in both of their responses. Obviously both girls were thinking of moving with us. This was a good sign.

"Yes!" confirmed the love of my life. "Your mother and I should both be able to relax a bit more if things go to plan."

"Well why on earth haven't you done it before now?" exclaimed Chaos. "It's quite obvious Mum isn't well, she's been self-medicating with caffeine and rubbish sugar products for far too long, and I bet you aren't much better. You have both been under too much pressure for too long. The human body isn't designed to cope with that. If there is a way out then you should take it. We all agree." She said this with a defiant confidence that hinted at lengthy chats with her siblings on this very subject.

"It's been well over a year since the rebuild was completed." Logic chimed in. "For goodness' sake, why have you waited until now to put the house on the market? There's no point in you grinding yourselves into the ground if there's an alternative."

Quiet shrugged, "It's a no brainer, Dad!"

Small nodded and said "Yuhpm!" emphatically, unintentionally punctuating his comment by spitting a few stray crumbs out of his bulging mouth. My subconscious mind vaguely noted that, somehow, the large, decorative serving plate that contained the remaining section of lemon drizzle cake had mysteriously moved so that it now sat squarely in front of my youngest child.

Beloved Husband turned to me with his blue eyes twinkling and smiled, asking, "Are you listening to them?"

"What do you mean?" asked Logic.

"Your mother has been worried that if we sell up it will break the ties that you girls have with your home. She is afraid that you won't want to come back if we move now that you've left home for university. That's why we've hung on for so long."

"You daft woman!" exclaimed Chaos with her usual delicacy, looking directly at me with her eyebrows raised.

"Yes. Where on earth did that come from Mum?" asked Logic.

"This is your home," I said, "it's where you grew up!"

"Yes it is," confirmed Chaos "and it has been really lovely growing up here, wobbly walls and all. But its people that count Mum, not bricks and mortar. If there's one thing the whole crumbly cottage thing taught us it's that! Just because we move somewhere different, this family is not going to fall apart. We'll still be us, just in a different house somewhere else. I know we're at uni now, and after that there will be the potential for jobs and stuff so who knows where we'll have to go for those, but we'll still come home. You're not going to get rid of us that easily you know. The vast majority of students move back home after college anyway. You do realise that don't you?"

"Come on mum," said Logic, "you've always told us that our strength comes from family. If the last few years haven't proved that to us then nothing will. House move, or no house move!"

Quiet cleared his throat and everyone looked at him, sensing that one of his carefully thought out and meaningful statements was imminent. Then in his lovely, deep voice he said slowly, "If we can live in a tent and a caravan together for over a year then I am pretty sure moving house will be a doddle!"

"MmmmHmm!" agreed Small chewing hard while dabbing his finger around the large (now empty) serving plate to make sure he hadn't missed any escaped cake crumbs.

"This is a gorgeous house Mum, but it's probably time for us to give it to someone else to enjoy; perhaps a family with little kids. They'll have a fab time growing up here just like we did but without the wobbly bit at the end. It's like magic here with the forest and the coast nearby. All the open space and fresh air. We've been so lucky."

I was quietly stunned. I had thought that they would just have bad memories. That all the good ones of the early years would be overshadowed by what had happened more recently, but it seemed that this was not the case. I am constantly amazed by the incredible resilience of youth! What amazing young people they are. It made me think that they could cope with anything life throws at them.

"Don't forget Mum," said Chaos, "We uni students are urban dwellers now. This is an opportunity for you to consider moving back towards civilisation. It's pretty amazing! There are all sorts of sophisticated things in the city, like street lights, pavements, mains drainage, gas pipes, public transport and night clubs."

"I'm not sure the parents will be too excited about night clubs Chaos!" said her sister, grinning at her.

"Ok maybe not night clubs, but you know what I mean," Chaos laughed. "This could be the start of a whole new adventure. But whatever we buy and wherever we buy it, I suggest we avoid 350 year old cob cottages. Ok?"

"Yeah!" they all chorused loudly and fell about laughing. Quiet had to quickly start bashing Small firmly between the shoulder blades because chuckling so hard had made him choke on his last mouthful of cake.

As Beloved Husband and I listened to the mayhem around us, he smiled at me and nudged my foot under the table in an 'I told you so' kind of way. Grinning slowly back at him, I could feel something tight and knotted, way down deep inside myself, suddenly start to unravel and float free. I should have trusted my beloved Barbarians more. It seemed they had no problems with the idea of moving onto the next stage in our lives together.

17: Ramification

Definition: a consequence that directly relates to an earlier decision

Returning to the past...

As is often the case, if you look closely at many disastrous situations you can usually find some sort of silver lining. Even if sometimes you have to look really, really hard.

The decision to take out the entire cob component of the house, while sadly, massively increasing the cost, had the beneficial effect of simplifying the job significantly in some very practical respects. There was now no possibility of salvaging the damaged floors and ceilings as these would need to be removed entirely. This would give us the opportunity to increase the ceiling heights of the downstairs rooms, which in their original incarnation had been quite low even before the walls had started to crumble.

Thor was able to set to on Monday morning and swing his adored sledgehammer to his heart's content, smashing and bashing at the ancient lathe and plaster partitions and wooden joists that divided up the internal space in the old cottage. He had a significantly less conservative approach to demolition than the other two builders. The main premise of his method seemed to involve randomly whacking things with all his might until they disappeared.

Destructive and very probably dangerous, he was nevertheless surprisingly effective and made short work of his clearance brief.

The roof was basically supported on three sides at this juncture as the new gable wall had set firmly by now and the undamaged second gable and back walls were still in situ. It was only the front wall that had stability issues and the builders wanted to use this time to install huge, industrial, ground to loft joist props to hold the roof more efficiently while the other three walls were to be systematically stripped out and rebuilt over modern foundations. This would be done one at a time in the same way that the new gable had been completed.

Skelly and I spent quite a lot of time watching this process over the coming weeks, as February trundled on towards March.

Unfortunately as February left so did Jack Frost. The beautifully crisp, fresh, cold weather was suddenly a thing of the past. You would think that we would be relieved that the true chill of winter was on its way out but it proved to be more of an out of the frying pan into the fire sort of a situation. The rain arrived with a vengeance in the first days of March and we began to realise how lucky we had been up until that point.

Hammering down in sheets with the wind adding force to the impact, the rainstorm started and simply didn't stop. A few days into the wet weather I noted that Skelly had acquired a golfing umbrella from somewhere, but Beloved Husband and the Barbarians denied all responsibility for its appearance.

The lads were working on the front of the house at this stage, having once again gone through the process of bringing down the damaged cob in careful sections.

Thank goodness for the thick plastic sheeting, that had been suspended from the roof plate to protect the walls four months previously, as the building team were able to pin the lower sections of these sheets away from the wall that was being dismantled to act as a kind of tent which enabled them to keep working. It kept the worst of the water off them but not all of it.

Once the removal of the old wall was complete, the builders must have been absolutely frozen digging the foundations for the new wall whilst standing knee deep in icy cold water. Surprisingly this didn't seem to bother them. They just turned the radio up and kept singing. I was amazed that they didn't develop trench-foot under the circumstances but they were indeed an impressively hardy bunch. I suppose it probably helped that they got to go home at the end of the day to nice warm houses to dry off and thaw out.

That was a luxury that unfortunately eluded us

With all that rain, came an invasion of mould.

It wasn't too bad in the house because we kept the fire going almost permanently and the space was quite well ventilated (there was a wall missing after all). Nevertheless, in the caravan I quickly noticed the steady creep of black fungus on both windows and walls which proved virtually impossible to keep at bay.

Unfortunately the built-in heating in the caravan didn't work at all. A friend had kindly lent us two portable oil storage radiators, the type that you plug into the mains electricity sockets. These operated independently via an internal thermostat and were quite effective at taking the chill off the air in the caravan.

However each trip to the house and back in the never ending rain brought water inside the caravan on coats, shoes and umbrellas which increased the damp atmosphere and eventually generated more and more condensation. Opening the window wasn't an option due to the weather, so it was a constant battle to wipe moisture from windows and walls on a daily basis in the hope that it would halt the pervasive progression of this insidious rot.

During that soggy spell we spent as much time in the house as possible, staying in the lounge area as late as possible in the evening before making a dash for the caravan in between the heaviest bursts of rain.

One evening I paused in the middle of clearing up the supper things in the kitchen and just watched my beloved Barbarians. Chaos was on her laptop, totally engrossed in whatever it was that she was typing so frantically (one of her books as it turned out), while nodding away to her music through her headphones. Logic was knitting something blue and fluffy and casting absent glances towards whatever Small was watching on TV. Quiet was engrossed in some sort of snapchat/messenger conversation with his school mates. All four were encased in thick fleece blankets on the sofas and the open fire was roaring away creating a cosy warm bubble.

I smiled at the scene they created, just as a small movement caught my eye. Adjusting my glasses and focussing hard on the carpet to the left of the fireplace. I could hardly believe my eyes. There in plain sight next to the log basket were three little field mice basking in the flickering glow from the flames.

The cat was comfortably ensconced on the coffee table and gave me a measured look as if to say, "I wouldn't bother if I were you." It was quite plain that she'd already spotted the encroaching wildlife and had no plans to do anything about them.

I sighed heavily. The mice were getting very brazen about sharing our living space now that it was so wet outside, but there was no way to stop them unfortunately. I had tried the humane mouse catchers but no matter how often I emptied the entrapped occupants out in the field next door they were often back in the house before I was. I absolutely refused to set real traps. Alive mice were bad enough but dead ones? No thank you!

I comforted myself with the knowledge that the caravan was wildlife-free, and at least we didn't have rats. Once the house was completely rebuilt it wouldn't be hard to evict all the additional, unwanted guests. They were only mice after all and they tended to stick to the warm hearth area, not venturing into the kitchen much at all. They probably knew better than to push their luck!

Nevertheless everything about our life at that point was made so much harder by the wet weather. For example changing the bedding in the caravan involved a massive effort on a weekly basis. (My one concession to luxury of any sort during those months had been to send the bedding out to the laundry to be washed and, more importantly, properly dried as it was simply impossible to achieve this anywhere in the house or caravan.)

While the beds themselves were actually quite small, the caravan rooms were equally tiny, which made the manoeuvres necessary to actually change the bed sheets very difficult, if not almost impossible.

In the case of Logic's bed (which, if you remember, was little more than a small double mattress crow-barred into a cupboard of similar dimensions) I had to scramble into the space by climbing on top of the mattress and then try to change it a section at a time whilst trying not to get in my own way. This involved peeling a bit of mattress away from the wall, hooking the sheet over it somehow and then letting both flop back into place against the wall again. It was rather like wrestling with an octopus. (Not that I have ever done that of course.) The other beds weren't much better. There just wasn't enough room to move. I suppose it did give me a good work out though, as I always needed a long sit down and a strong cup of tea after the job was done.

It wasn't long though before I noticed that sheets, duvets and pillows were starting to speckle with mildew when I did the weekly change and I knew that it was definitely not good for the Barbarians' health to be sleeping in such damp conditions. All we needed at that point, to really finish us off, was someone to get ill. In fact, I was surprised to note that, so far, we seemed to have escaped the worst of the winter bugs that were floating around that year, which was a small mercy but a very welcome one.

Just as I was formulating a plan to avoid the mould by moving us all back into the lounge to sleep on the floor by the open fire in the house, as we had done before the caravan had arrived, the wet weather finally broke. The sledging rainstorms that were arriving with relentlessly regularity, one after another, suddenly stopped. It was as if someone had finally remembered to turn off a gushing tap and then the sun came out, bright, warm and so very welcome. What a transformation it was.

At last, April had arrived, as had what was to be the warmest Easter on record for many years. If someone was watching over us they had obviously realised that we needed a break.

Everybody's spirits started to lift just a little bit higher with each day of sunshine that followed. The girls' A and AS level exam revision could now take place out on the patio on loungers in bright beaming sunshine. At the same time the boy Barbarians could resume their life-long quest to cause benevolent, physical damage to each other via spectacular rugby and football related tackles, outside, where I didn't have to watch them while they did it. I was also grateful to note the trio of friendly field mice sneaking out of the open patio doors and heading back into the wild.

Meanwhile the builders could dry their boots off and shed their many layers of ratty jumpers. Skelly put away his brolly and acquired a pair of shades, while the repair job at the front of the house progressed ever onwards.

The extraction of the cob was a very painful thing to watch, especially once the team had moved onto the two undamaged walls. Beloved Husband and I had fallen in love with this little cottage precisely because of the beautiful mix of over three centuries of history that she represented. I felt like such a failure that the original seventeenth century walls were being removed on our watch. It seemed somehow sacrilegious to be dismantling something that had stood for so long. Yet what choice did we have?

It became obvious that the people who had built her all those years ago had used pretty much anything that came their way in the creation of those old walls. Lofty and Shy Guy, who continued with their carefully systematic carving up of the cob into manageable chunks with the pneumatic drill, frequently presented me with their finds. A chipped pottery jug, some blunt and useless, abandoned tools and a broken, wooden broom handle were all found entombed within the cob as it came apart. Shy Guy took great delight in each new discovery and spent so much time carefully extracting them that he could have been auditioning for a part on Time Team.

It was such a shame we didn't come across a chest of lost jewels or other such valuable hidden treasure that might cover some of the cost of the bills to come, but never mind. Such a discovery would no doubt slow things down and cause complications anyway. The last thing we needed was to have a visit from the county archaeologist forced on us by the council to delay things, especially if we were then made to donate any such discovery to the British Museum rather than auction it off to the highest bidder. Yes I am not ashamed to admit to a few mercenary tendencies! I am only human after all!

With the advent of the lovely dry, sunny weather it wasn't long before the main structure of the new front wall was in place and ready to take a share of the weight of the roof while the second gable wall was taken down. This gable consisted of a massive inglenook fireplace and the associated chimney breast with its ancient foot and hand holds that stretched right up inside.

Work on this wall had to take place on the inside of the cottage as the other side of the second cob gable wall was yet another small, single story extension. This structure, like the back section of the house that was now part of the kitchen, had been built in the 1900's. We were hoping that, like the back section, it had been built independently too, with a small gap between the two structures meaning that the cob could be removed without causing any problems.

I found it absolutely heart breaking to watch this part of the cob being taken apart, as the large, inglenook fireplace was my absolute favourite feature of the whole house. Nevertheless as it came down it was to reveal a hidden secret that we could not possibly have predicted.

As Lofty and Shy Guy were systematically cutting up this section of cob there was a thunderous crash followed by sudden shouts of fear and the two of them came haring out of the cottage as if Beelzebub and all the hounds of hell were chasing them.

Startled, I leapt up from my spot in the sunshine on the bench next to Skelly and ran towards them. "What is it?" I asked.

Both were panting heavily and wide eyed with shock. Lofty pointed back towards the house and said "It's huge! I only had seconds to recognise what it was. I've seen one before but never that big... and then we just ran, but none of them.... well.....I don't think any of them are alive... its...horrible..." he tailed off with a shudder, bending over and putting his hands on his knees as he tried to slow his breathing.

Thor and I looked at each other intrigued. How interesting! Had we stumbled across some dead bodies? Please don't tell me there had been a murder and we needed to call the coroner! Not wanting to sounds unsympathetic here, of course, but that really would chuck a spanner in the works and delay things massively.

All the noise and yelling had alerted the Barbarians to a potential disaster and soon Logic was sprinting round from the back of the house armed with a first aid kit, although what use she thought it would be if any of our builders had actually been crushed to death I wasn't too sure. I admired her optimism that an antibacterial wipe, a few sticky plasters and a sling might be all we needed.

Chaos followed in her wake, very sensibly clutching a mobile phone (presumably in case we needed to call an ambulance) and an ice pack. Even the boys had peeled themselves away from the PlayStation and wandered round to see what the kerfuffle was all about.

Anyway, back to the dead bodies...

Gesturing for the Barbarians to stay well back I moved cautiously towards the house and peered through the gap where the door would eventually go and looked at what was left of the old fireplace.

Wow!

It took me a few moments to work out what it was that I was looking at, but when we did… well! Forget the coroner! I rather thought we ought to be ringing David Attenborough!

Behind the chimney breast, between the old cob and the wall of the 1900's extension there was approximately a five centimetre gap from ground to roof. A large section of cob had fallen away, which had revealed an enormous wasps' nest filling the entirety of this gap. It was absolutely huge!

No doubt it had proven to be a fabulously warm and protected location behind the almost constantly operational fireplace. Lofty and Shy Guy had been quite right to run. Had this been an active nest they would no doubt have been on the receiving end of a mammoth angry swarm. No wonder they looked alarmed. My little bottle of Piriton wouldn't have been much help against a million or more wasp stings.

Fortunately for us all this nest was an abandoned one, apart from a few desiccated corpses. Even so it was unexpectedly beautiful close up, if a bit creepy. A most impressive structure indeed, but I am glad I hadn't known it was there in all the years we had lived in the cottage. Ignorance is bliss in these circumstances I feel.

Given the shaky state of two of my poor builders we rather felt it was time for some tea and biscuits Logic took the (thankfully not needed) first aid kit back to the kitchen and filled the kettle. I didn't really think that any of the builders should be back in charge of the pneumatic drill until they had calmed down.

So Lofty and Shy Guy sat down next to Skelly on the bench to wait for refreshments whilst Thor went back to what was left of the inglenook fireplace to do what he does best. He bashed and smashed about with his sledgehammer removing all traces of the wasps' nest so that his comrades could carry on with their demolition job when they were ready. After a restorative cup of tea and large plate of chocolate cookies, they both felt much better and the rest of the wall came down with no further drama.

18: Perseverance

Definition: the determination to keep doing something even though it proves hard or difficult. Not giving up in the face of failure.

Returning to the present day ...

A few days after the girls had returned to their temporary university homes I was thinking about my unplanned taekwondo taster session and then my enjoyable evening with the local WI ladies. It occurred to me that I had experienced several more good nights' sleep in a row. It was getting quite addictive, this restful sleep lark, I rather enjoyed it. I found myself completing my daily fine motor skills exercises with a smile on my face. The radio warbled away to itself in the corner and I occasionally sipped at my hot water and lemon juice without noticing the absence of caffeine. Important progress, I felt, added to which I was pleased to see some not insignificant improvement in my fine brush control.

In view of how much fun my unexpected introduction to martial arts had been, I had decided not to do Quiet any actual bodily harm. He had unwittingly done me a favour, but I wasn't going to give him too much credit for it because he would never let me forget it. Even so, I had decided to go to the junior taekwondo session later on that week.

Beloved Husband was surprisingly not keen on my choice of preferred exercise class and kept suggesting alternatives. Obviously he was ok with the idea of a wife who does yoga but not so much ok with one who does martial arts. Interesting!

Once we had firmly established that I was going to go back to taekwondo whether he liked it or not, he decided to come with me, saying that he was worried I might get hurt. I think it more likely that he had clocked just how many fit (yes, I do mean *that* sort of 'fit' this time) fellas there were at the class and felt a teeny, tiny bit insecure. Although, it is far more likely that he just liked the idea of a couple of pints in the bar afterwards! Either way I was pleased he was coming too. It would be fun to do something together.

Spurred on by their father's resolution, or possibly the thought of being allowed to legitimately kick each other in public without being told off, both boys declared an interest too so there were going to be quite a few more novices in the junior class that week. I smiled looking forward to it, which in itself was a measure of how significantly less anxious I was.

Why wasn't I worrying about the boys getting injured? Or even my Beloved Husband?

Maybe I was finally getting the hang of chilling out.

In the meantime there had been a couple of telephone calls for me but I had missed them. Quiet had taken messages for me and muttered something about exhibitions. He had scribbled a telephone number and a name down on the back of an old envelope. He kept nagging me to call the lady back but I never seemed to have the time. He was right though, but don't tell him I said so, it was time to sell some of my used canvas collection. I just wasn't sure that I wanted to get back into the world of exhibiting. So much effort went into each show but I wasn't entirely sure that it was worth it.

Nevertheless there was no doubt that if I agreed to do an exhibition it would cheer Beloved Husband up no end, because he could have one or two of his sheds back. It would also stop Quiet making sly little digs about my fish painting 'obsession'. (Philistine!)

I heard the clang of the letterbox, signalling that the postman had been. Today was obviously one of the random two days a week that we were a scheduled part of his route. You don't get post every day when you live on the backside of beyond. That was something that would change if we successfully sold the house and returned to civilisation.

I shoved that whole exhibition issue from my mind and went to pick up the sealed and stamped envelopes that now littered the floor just inside the front door, spotting immediately that there was an intriguing little parcel for me. Smiling contentedly to myself I ambled into the kitchen and tore open my package to find that Logic had sent me a little plastic bag containing a muslin pouch full of what looked like very suspicious herbs. Hmmm!?!

My heart flipped over as my brain immediately leapt to entirely the wrong conclusion! Please don't tell me my smart mathematician daughter had fallen into the wrong crowd and started experimenting with dodgy substances? She's only been a student five minutes! (OK, six months to be exact, so plenty of time really.) More to the point, why on earth was she sending this stuff to me? I know we are lucky enough to have a very close mother-daughter relationship but she must realise that sending me illegal drugs through the post was pushing the boundaries a bit surely? Not to mention quite risky. I know how nosy people can get in the queue for the village post office now that you have to say exactly what's in your parcel at the counter. I'm as bad as anyone else, mind, you just can't help earwigging when you're standing waiting in line. Every time I want to send a package now and I have to declare what's in it, I am tempted to make up something outrageous just to entertain the person behind me; but I don't think it would ever occur to me to suggest I might be posting marijuana. Hmmm!

Quickly scanning the little note she included in the parcel I soon gave a sigh of relief. Apparently the little muslin twist was a type of herbal tea bag, a gift from her friend the hippy down the hall. Now, I appreciate that this doesn't completely rule out suspicious substances, but, from what Logic has told me about this new friend, she is a vegan and treats her body like a temple. Something I should really consider doing one day when I have the time. Not that I could ever be bothered with all that faddy 'clean eating' the newspapers were banging on about, which is just as well, because they seem to have back-tracked lately and are now saying it's not good for you at all. I am glad I didn't waste my time.

Logic wrote that when she had told her friend that I was trying to go completely caffeine-free but hated herbal teas, the Helpful Hippy had insisted that I was obviously drinking the wrong type and was no doubt making it the wrong way too. She had included detailed, written instructions from the Hippy on just how to make a good cup of herbal tea. By the time the kettle had boiled I had educated myself appropriately and made my first cup of surprisingly pleasant smelling blackcurrant and vanilla herbal tea. Perhaps the she might be right after all.

Unfortunately the Hippy ended her little note with the advice that if I really wanted to go caffeine-free I was going to have to give up chocolate completely and kindly suggested several alternatives that were available from most health food shops.

Like that was ever happening! Anyway, I was starting to feel better already so there was no need to go completely overboard.

While I drank my herbal tea, I rattled off an email to Logic to thank her friend for the tea bag and the advice and, mentally crossing my fingers behind my back, I promised I would think about giving up chocolate. Then, tea break over, I headed upstairs to change the beds.

PART 5

Every new beginning comes from some other beginning's end.

Seneca 54 AD

19: Resurgence

Definition: a significant increase in activity after a period of reduced action.

Back to the crumbly cottage and a disgustingly early morning in the past…

I rubbed my eyes and stared at the wall of green boxes in front of me. I seriously hadn't had enough sleep for this.

I couldn't really blame Beloved Husband for the fact that we had woken up ridiculously early again. Now that the weather was improving and the mornings were getting lighter earlier, the dawn chorus was starting to crank up in the really small hours again and the dance routine of the sprightly sparrows on the metal caravan roof was getting more adventurous. You would think that we would have gotten used to the noise by now, but the random nature of the scratchy, hoppity skips and jumps proved impossible to tune out. Not so for the Barbarians it would seem, as they usually managed to slumber on determinedly until lunchtime given half a chance.

Nevertheless I could (and did) blame Beloved Husband for dragging me out of bed and off to a garden centre on the first Saturday morning that it wasn't teaming down with rain. Seriously, I didn't even know they opened this early. I could have been having a nice, cosy lie in with a cup of tea and a book, yet here I was looking at …. Well!…. Surely not! I rubbed my eyes yet again and scrutinised the shelving unit before me in disbelief.

Then I gave Beloved Husband what can only be described as a *speaking look*. It was saying quite a lot to him, along the lines of: 'Are you seriously asking me what type of grass seed to buy?' Among other less polite things, if you get my drift.

Obviously, as a method of communication, this look was fairly effective because he gave a sheepish grin, shrugged, grabbed the nearest box and said, "OK, fair enough, I'll just get this one then....or maybe...um..." Looking at me again he hastily exchanged his selection for another almost identical box, and declared, "This is the one we need. It's perfect!" At last! He had chosen a huge box of grass seed from the wall of indistinguishable alternatives and then we set off for the plant section.

Now it should be noted here that I don't really *do* gardens. Don't get me wrong, I like them, but I don't actually *garden* if I can help it. Fortunately Beloved Husband does and it was actually rather nice to see him so cheerful after the last few months of doom and gloom. Now that the sun had returned he was no longer obsessing about the building site at the front of our house because he could focus on the wilderness at the back. Admittedly it was getting a touch untidy. The emergent growth of the new spring would soon over run us if he didn't exert a little control, but I loved the bright succession of natural beauty that was unfolding with the new season. It began with snowdrops and was rapidly followed by daffodils, bluebells, buttercups and daisies; a promise of the coming summer which filled me with so much hope. Although I did have a little sympathy for Beloved Husband as I could see he was itching to get going with lawn mower, and hedge trimmer.

This morning's little trip was to find grass seed to repair the huge tracks of damaged lawn in the back garden created during the installation of the static caravan last September. He hadn't had the heart to do anything about the damage at the time which just goes to show how devastated he was by the whole house falling down fiasco. So it was nice to see a bit more of a spring in his step. (No seasonal pun intended!) Although I personally felt we should leave the damaged area well alone because the caravan was going to have to go back out the way it came in, eventually. No doubt causing just as much damage as it passed. I didn't mention that though, I didn't want to think just how long it would be until that might happen. If Beloved Husband wanted to plant grass seed, then grass seed he could plant. Who was I to get in his way?

It has become quite apparent over the last 21 years that my Beloved Husband and I have wildly different approaches to the garden. He usually launches himself enthusiastically into the great outdoors intending to assert his dominance over nature, with the help of various petrol driven implements such as the chain saw and the leaf blower. Although, we haven't got as far as a ride-on lawn mower yet, much to my surprise.

I, on the other hand, always enter the garden with the sole purpose of sitting down, preferably with a cup of tea and a jolly good book! So I am not really sure why he seemed to think I even wanted to come to the garden centre with him this morning. But here I was and, having selected the chosen grass seed, we were apparently now off to buy some sort of flowering stuff.

Later on that day, it became patently obvious to me that the cup of tea/book option still wasn't on the agenda. As I was approaching my favourite rattan patio chair, Beloved Husband waltzed purposefully past on his way to select his weapon of choice from the garage. Pausing dramatically, he nodded disdainfully at the patio planters and suggested in a polite but firm voice that I might like to 'do' something about them.

Hmmmmm!!!! Really?? Would I?

Let me think......

'Nope not really' was the immediate response that sprang to mind, but I could tell from the expression on his face that such a retort wasn't going to be received terribly well. So, for a quiet life, I rolled up my sleeves and got stuck in. It's amazing what you can achieve in a short period of time when you really put your mind to it. I made quick work of dealing with the dismal-looking and very dead whatever-it-was he planted last year and instead installed the dainty, emergent dahlias we had selected from the garden centre that morning.

When Beloved Husband returned an hour later (having beaten the early spring growth of grass into submission) the pots looked beautiful as I serenely turned the pages of my book and sipped nonchalantly from my mug of coffee. I have to confess that I had my fingers crossed that the dahlias would survive, as I had been somewhat brusque with them. I don't really have a good gardening track record. So far the only things I've managed to nurture with any success in my life are my four Barbarians and they seem to be surviving in spite of me, not because of me. They grow like weeds, especially the boy ones. Perhaps I should plant weeds!

Narrowing his eyes suspiciously at the speed with which I had achieved my allotted task, Beloved Husband obviously came to the conclusion that letting sleeping dogs lie (or rather leaving reading wives alone to get on with it) was probably his best approach at that moment in time. He is a wise man on occasion. Shaking his head in exasperation he headed off no doubt to find a sharp and dangerous toy to play with.

As I sat there sipping my coffee my attention wandered from my book and I couldn't help but remember some of the fun times we had had in this garden with the Barbarians as they had grown up. There was one particular summer when they had discovered Lara Croft and the Tomb Raider films and as a result Beloved Husband was over the moon. At last Disney had been banished and the Barbarians were starting to watch the sort of films he enjoyed too. Soon it would be Lethal Weapon and Die Hard!

Having watched all three Tomb Raider movies in one weekend, he and the Barbarians let their imaginations roam free as they developed their own version of the story in the back garden with loaded water pistols and holsters strapped to each thigh. In addition a serious, homemade assault course was constructed in the garden as part of the adventure.

With hindsight, the combination of a rope swing, a tractor tyre tunnel, a wobbly balance beam, a rusty climbing frame and an over excited nearly forty year-old is obviously an accident waiting to happen. Fortunately the inevitable ensuing trip to casualty, with Beloved Husband's ankle encased in frozen peas, proved to be just as entertaining for our hardy horde of Barbarians, because we were there for quite some time. Thankfully I was able to persuade them that shooting the other patients with their water pistols wouldn't be very sporting so they just concentrated on 'poor Daddy'!

Heaven only knows what the casualty officer thought we had been up to though. I did try to brush everyone down before we went in but when you've been fighting enemy Tomb Raiders all morning you don't generally look terribly presentable. All those commando rolls and fighting your way through hedges etc... There were streaks of mud and twigs in all sorts of random places.

Eventually we returned home with our wounded hero even though he had significant difficulty in believing that the ankle wasn't actually broken. It hurt! The x-ray must have missed something!

Having installed him on the sofa and administered a hefty dose of pain killers and some fresh cool packs, we decided to feed him a lot of ice cream to cheer him up and then watched all the films again just to make sure we hadn't missed anything important the first time around. Obviously the Barbarians and I kindly helped him to eat the ice cream while we were watching.

***

Now, while all the messing around (sorry, gardening) at the back of the house was going on, the building team at the front were making amazing progress. It wasn't long before we had four solid walls, all built to modern specifications.

Only four short weeks after the sunshine arrived so did the Easter holidays and by then we were all able to safely stand inside the front section of our home and stare in awe right up to the inside of the roof ridge.

Genuine Old Building Expert had checked the work over extremely thoroughly that morning and given us a massive 'thumbs up' with a huge smile on his face. Master Roofer had also popped by to give the roof a once over and concluded that it was still in excellent condition in spite of all the shenanigans that had gone on beneath it.

There was no longer any need for steels and props to hold the roof up. Incredible! Our new walls with their fabulous foundations were perfectly capable of doing the job themselves. We still had a long way to go, as there were no internal walls, joists or ceilings and no floor, first story, staircase, windows, lights, heating, or front door to speak of yet, but we had walls! Progress! Yay!

No more nights lying awake worrying that there would be a colossal crash telling us that the roof had given way to gravity at last or had even been blown clean off in the wind. We could lie awake worrying about other stuff, but not that, which was a massive load off our minds.

The Boss made one of his visits to apprise us of the next stage of the project and to warn us of the likely costs that would ensue. We had to swallow hard at the figures but had no choice other than to agree that the cottage needed a floor. We couldn't continue to live over bare earth now that we knew that it was there. Building regulations wouldn't sign the job off if we didn't put a modern standard floor in. It wasn't The Boss' fault that he had to be the bearer of bad news in the form of costings and he obviously took no delight in it. Nevertheless his advice was sound so we braced ourselves and agreed to the work needed for the floor.

Two days later we watched together as the building team took delivery of the dinkiest little, hired, mini digger we had ever seen. This machine was so tiny that it could be driven through the gap left in the front wall where a porch (with a front door) would eventually be built. As this new section of the house didn't have a first floor in place yet, the lads could use the digger to quickly remove the earth floor down to a suitable depth to lay a modern, insulated, damp proofed, concrete floor.

It goes without saying that everyone wanted a turn operating the little digger. Especially Small!

I came home from work later that day after the lads had gone home, to find Skelly firmly ensconced at the controls with a crook-lock jammed through both the steering wheel and his lower rib cage. Apparently Beloved Husband felt that he would act as a deterrent to stop any one wandering down the lane from the nearby village pub and having a go on the dinky digger after closing time.

Not a bad call!

20: Transfiguration

Definition: a total change in form or look to a more enhanced or spiritual condition.

The present is looking brighter....

Now that I was sleeping regularly, I was starting to wake up with more energy. I sometimes willingly sprang out of bed at 6am ready to get on with my day, much to Beloved Husband's utter disgust. That morning, having taken a sneaky degree of pleasure in *accidentally* waking him up even if it was only momentarily before he dropped back off to sleep, I scurried downstairs in his dressing gown (it's warmer than mine) and dived into my studio. I found I had been dreaming of the beautiful spring flowers that had grown around the caravan while we had been living in the garden and I had awoken with a new painting planned out in my mind. I wanted to get a start on it before I had to go to work.

This was going to be quite an ambitious piece and would involve some of the new techniques I had been working on as a result of the good doctor's suggestion that I adapt the way I work. I knew exactly how I want to approach this painting because I had dreamt about the process over and over all night.

Dragging a large, square, stretched canvas out of the studio and into the kitchen I laid it on the stone floor on top of some newspaper. I knew that I was about to annoy the entire family, because what I did next was going to mean they would all have to tip toe carefully past this wet canvas, whilst trying to find breakfast and get ready for school.

However that didn't stop me, they know what I am like and I really needed a wide flat surface that could be wiped down afterwards. The kitchen floor was perfect.

I armed myself with paint, PVA glue, a four inch brush and loads of tissue paper. Switching on the kettle first so that a hot cup of something wasn't long away I opened the PVA and poured it all over the bottom third of the canvas, smearing it around with the big brush to get complete coverage. Scrunching up the tissue paper I then layered it over the glue base and moved it around gently. Tweaking and pushing, sometimes tearing the fragile fabric, I made what would eventually be an intentionally textured surface when the glue finally dried. Then mixing more PVA with generous quantities of dark green acrylic paint I slathered this all over the top of the tissue paper, making sure that every single speck of canvas was covered. Just as I was standing up having completed my mission Beloved Husband stumbled down the stairs and ground to a halt when he saw what I was up to.

"Seriously?" he asked with a rumpled grin. "This is why you bounced out of bed so early? What are you on?"

I smiled happily and leaned over the wet canvas to pass him a cup of tea before pouring hot water on my own herbal tea bag. "Well not caffeine anymore!" I declared. "I feel great. This is going to take all day to dry before I can do the next stage, so I thought it made sense to get it done first thing. I'll be able to work on it upright in the studio after that."

"Hmmm! Of course! That makes perfect sense," he muttered a touch sarcastically before asking, "Have you got paint on my dressing gown again?"

I quickly rolled up the cuff and smiled brightly, "No! Of course not!" It'll wash out. Hopefully!

He stepped back towards the stairs and yelled up them, "Boys! Be careful when you come into the kitchen, your mother's at it again."

There were several dramatic groans from upstairs but I ignored them. I had just realised that I had literally painted myself into a bit of a corner and would have to go out of the conservatory doors and walk round to the front of the house in my dressing gown to come back in the front door to reach the stairs and my bedroom to get dressed for work. Oh how I suffer for my art! Beaming cheerfully at Beloved Husband as he wrestled with the bread bin and the toaster, which were fortunately on his side of the huge wet canvas, I set off with my brush and paint pots intending to wash them out using the tap by the garage on my trip round to the front of the house.

Eventually, after depositing clean painting equipment back in my little studio, I headed up to take a quick shower when I bumped into Quiet as he came out of his bedroom stifling a yawn.

"So!" he said with a long-suffering sigh, "what are you painting this time? No! Let me guess, more…."

"Nope!" I answered triumphantly. "No fish. You'll see."

"Can't wait!" he murmured sarcastically under his breath as he stumbled down the stairs in search of a cereal fix.

***

A short while later, while on the way to work, having delivered the boy Barbarians to school, my phone sprang into life. Fortunately Beloved Husband had set up the hands free gadget in my car for me so that I could safely answer it. If he hadn't I would have spent the whole journey worrying which of the Barbarians had met with some catastrophic accident and needed me, but obviously not daring to pick up the phone and answer it while driving, in case I caused a catastrophic accident of my own.

Luckily there was a supermarket carpark just ahead where I could pull in and park up so I could concentrate. Pressing the button on the steering wheel to answer the call, I was both concerned to register Chaos' voice but simultaneously relieved to hear that she sounded fine. "Are you alright?" I asked. I was puzzled as to why she might be ringing me this early. It was only half past eight in the morning. Surely she should either be dashing to a lecture or fast asleep like any normal student.

"Of course I am!" she replied indignantly.

"Good!" I said and waited.

There was a crackly silence.

"Was there something you wanted?" I asked eventually.

"Just checking you are OK," she said somewhat defensively.

“Chaos!” I said sternly, “What is this about? I’m on my way to work and I am going to be late. You are going to have to be more specific!”

There was a pause and then, “I had a message from Quiet….and….well… actually he’s a bit worried about you.”

“Really, why?”

“He said you’re painting dark stuff again.”

“Yes, I was this morning,” I agreed. “What’s the problem?”

“He thinks he’s upset you. Apparently he said something to you about your last painting. Um…rainbows or unicorns or something? Anyway he says he didn’t mean it, he was only teasing you but now he says you’re painting in really dark colours again. A big canvas. Like last time, when you were… you know…” she trailed off uncertainly.

I laughed, “Ha! He thinks he’s tipped me over into a major depression with his jokey comments doesn’t he? Serves him right! He shouldn’t tease his poor old mum. Text him back and tell him I’m fine. Never better in fact.”

“OK, are you sure?”

“Absolutely!” I replied, “I feel fine! Don’t worry about me.” I didn’t like to mention the minor episode of palpitations I had experienced whilst in the shower that morning. It was only a small one and passed relatively quickly. Other than that, I really did feel fine.

"That's great!" she said with enthusiasm before continuing, "and the dark canvas?"

"Don't worry it's only a base for something. I plan to cheer it up significantly this evening if it's dry."

"OK good. Well you certainly sound much better to me. I'll tell him not to worry."

"You do that, now I've got to get to work OK? I'd better go. Let's chat tonight."

"Sure! OK! Take care! Bye!"

The phone connection dropped off and the radio came back on as I pulled out of the carpark and headed for work. I hummed cheerfully along to it as I threaded my way through the morning traffic. Ten minutes later I neatly squeezed my little purple car into the last parking space outside the office before heading inside to pick my way through the pile of paperwork on my desk.

21: Evolution

***Definition**: the gradual change of something from simple to more complex.*

Back at the building site in the past...

I admit it! I talk to myself. Many people would think that suggests I might be a little bit mad.

I don't know if you are the same, but as a multi-tasking mother I often feel that no one is listening to me, so by talking to myself I am at least guaranteed one attentive audience member.

So there I was one day, in the kitchen, chatting away to myself when I spotted the most enormous spider. You know the sort, with hairy legs and big, black boots! Now, I am not a fan of spiders it must be said, but with the sheer number sharing our crumbly residence at that time I had had no choice but to get used to them popping up all over the place. Rather than continue talking to myself I often started talking to my eight legged companions instead. Usually I was asking them politely if they minded just staying where they were and not scurrying around in that jerky, jumpy spider-like way they have.

Usually those conversations ran along the following sorts of lines:

"Oh! Hello nice Mr Spider, you gave me a shock! I didn't see you there. Tell you what you just stay still over there where I can see you ... and I'll carry on doing what I am doing over here .... and we won't have a problem......OK?"

You get the general idea I am sure.

So there I was one day muttering away to Sammy, (Yes I gave them all names too – it helped make them more approachable, along with the assumption that they understood English!) when I heard a gentle cough coming from the direction of the patio doors. Taking my eyes of my amiable arachnid for a split second or two, I saw that Thor had trotted around from the building site at the front of the house with a tray of empty tea cups. From the puppy-dog look on his face he was obviously after more caffeine. He had thoughtfully taken off his muddy boots and was shuffling across the stone floor in his (not very clean) socks to deposit the tray by the sink for me.

Now that the rain had stopped, it was a really hot, sunny day outside and I noticed that Thor had taken off his shirt. (Settle down! He is far too young for me and I am a married woman!) From a purely artistic point of view, I couldn't help but take benign note of his bulging biceps and impressive six pack as well as the intricately decorative tattoos he had on display. I suddenly realised quite why so many of Chaos and Logic's friends from sixth form were making the effort to walk, cycle and sometimes even hitch lifts over to our house to do their A-level revision.

Their earnest claims that it is so quiet and peaceful for revision out here in the country hadn't really rung terribly true, but I hadn't pursued the matter. After all this place is not much more than a construction site with the radio blaring full volume and three beefy builders singing their hearts out (with varying degrees of accuracy) all day!

But I digress… back to Thor and the, now, confused look on his face as he realised I was talking to someone that he couldn't see.

"Hi!" I said brightly.

"Hi!" he replied, smiling cautiously and looking round to see who else was there. "Sorry to interrupt, I thought you took the kids to school."

"I did!" I confirmed.

"So who are you talking to then?" he asked.

I nodded towards Sammy. "Him!"

Thor's eyes followed my gaze up to the corner of the kitchen ceiling.

"Ah!" he said nodding slowly. Then after a pause he looked back at me and said, "Why?"

"Because he might stay where he is if I do." I replied sheepishly realising how daft this sounded. "I don't really like spiders, I can cope with smaller ones but he is a bit too big for me."

Thor considered this for a minute then nodded as if this were a perfectly reasonable response. Then flicking his long blonde hair over his shoulder, manfully, he nodded at Sammy and said, "Want me to get rid of it for you?"

"Yes, but please don't kill him," I said hastily, having visions of Thor fetching his sledge hammer. "I don't want to hurt him particularly, I would just prefer he was somewhere else."

"Fair enough!" he replied with a nod and he reached up, cupped his hands around the huge spider and gently carried him outside, walking right over to the garden boundary in his socks, before reaching down and tipping Sammy into the long grass of the field beyond the fence.

Coming back into the kitchen he seemed deep in thought for a moment before eventually looking at me and saying carefully, "You do realise he'll probably be back, don't you?"

"Oh, I know, but I'll worry about that tomorrow. There's quite a lot of additional wildlife in this house now because of all the months we have spent with broken walls. I am getting used to it, but I am looking forward to when we can sort all that out, after the rebuild is finished. It won't be a problem for ever. Now, how about I bring you guys round a tray of fresh tea as a thank you for rescuing me?"

He smiled and nodded his thanks "That would be great, Thanks. The concrete for the new floor is down now. It just needs to set. We're going to finish off the porch walls next and then that'll be our bit of the job over and we'll leave you in peace. The chippies will be starting as soon as the floor is dry enough to walk on."

I hadn't realised that the team would be changing but I suppose it was obvious really. These guys specialised in concrete and brick work and the next stage would require skilled wood workers. It was a fantastic step forward. They would start to reconstruct the inside of our home and put in ceilings, stud walls and stairs. We were making amazing progress, but as I watched Thor shuffling back across the stone floor to the doors and slipping his boots back on, I realised I would be sorry to see them go.

While the kettle came to the boil I dug in the tins to find the latest batch of chocolate chip cookies the girls had whipped up last night. Knights in shining armour deserved cookies after rescuing damsels in distress from big fat spiders I felt, so I put some on the tray and headed round to deliver the refreshments and check out my new concrete floor.

Handing out the drinks and cookies I noticed Thor scrabbling around on the floor just inside the half-finished porch. He spotted me and gesturing at the floor he said "Look! It's a present from us to you, to say thank you for all the tea!"

I went over and looked down at a cartoon of a smiling spider with long legs and big boots carefully carved into the semi-wet cement of the new floor.

"This one will stay right here and not move a muscle, I promise!" said Thor with a chuckle. "Even when the carpenters lay that wooden floor you've chosen over him, you'll know exactly where he is. Standing guard!"

I couldn't help grinning back at him and asked, "Will he tell all the other spiders to stay away?"

"Absolutely!"

I laughed, I was definitely going to miss these guys.

22: Purgatory

Definition: a place of extreme suffering where one expiates ones sins

Back to the mother juggling jobs in the present...

Fortunately the work day passed quickly and it wasn't long before I was picking my boy Barbarians up from their schools and dropping them at their chosen after school activities. I just had time to pop home and check on the progress of my drying canvas before I had to go back and retrieve them.

Fortunately the gluey, dark green base was almost dry, so it would not be long before I could start the next stage of my painting. Noting in passing that there didn't seem to be much in the way of any edible items in either the fridge or the cupboards, I headed straight back out to raid the supermarket on my way to the school.

Once home again, laden with basic food supplies, I was able to pick up the canvas and lean it against the wall near the patio doors so that it was out of the way while I unpacked the shopping and started to cook dinner. I couldn't wait to get on with painting but I made myself mentally run through all the practical things I would have to get sorted out first, like feeding the hungry horde, sorting out some washing before it spilled out of the utility room and buried us all alive and.... oh no! A sixth sense made me check the family calendar.... parent's evening! Oh heck, I'd forgotten about that!

Heart sinking, I realised that I wasn't going to be able to paint that evening at all. It would be too late by the time I got back, the light would be all wrong. I could feel my spirits dropping down into my boots with the disappointment. Damn! If it wasn't bad enough that I had all this washing to do, I was now going to have to attend the scrum that the local primary school called parent's evening as well.

Going on the experience of previous years, this would generally involve all the parents for a particular year group being herded into the centre of the main school hall, with all the tired looking teachers sitting behind desks set out around the edge. I was never quite sure if this particular arrangement was so that the teachers could get a better view of the parents as they politely pushed, delicately elbowed and sometimes actively flailed fists to get past each other, in order to be first to park their bums on one of the two seats set out in front of their preferred teacher, so that they could discuss 'Little Johnny's' progress.

It was a very educational experience in more ways than one, even though it was utter torture for both parents and teachers. I found it quite amazing that there were always some parents with such an inflated sense of self-importance who refused to pay any attention to the list of appointment times which had all been carefully booked up in the preceding week. These parents would simply barge their way to the front of any vaguely polite queue that the other (more reasonable) parents were trying to stick to.

It should be remembered that there were over 100 pupils in each primary school year. One must also keep in mind, the fact that the staff had already done a full day's work keeping all those pupils alive, under control and hopefully educating them at the same time. Given that fact, I would be very surprised if any of the teachers I managed to get near that evening could remember their own name let alone that of their students. In fact one year I was so exhausted by the time I got to the teacher that I didn't notice for the first three minutes that she was talking about someone else's child. As that other child was handing in their homework on time and generally doing very well I decided that was good enough for me. I didn't have the energy to correct the mistake.

Nevertheless, no matter how much I hated these evenings, if I wished to consider myself a good parent, and didn't want the school to note my absence and inevitably draw unflattering conclusions, I was going to have to attend.

Checking the communal diary on my phone I was not surprised to see that Beloved Husband conveniently had a late meeting at work scheduled in for this evening. I couldn't help but surmise that he had clocked the date of parents' evening well before I had, and made sure he had a reason not to be available! A very small part of me applauded his ingenuity.

Considering the hell I now realised I was facing for the evening, I wondered if I was brave enough to suggest that it was time the boys learned how to use the washing machine. This might mean that I didn't have to do all that washing by myself, but I decided that I couldn't quite bring myself to unleash that particular monster. My poor machine was only hanging on by the merest thread as it was, so letting the boys loose on it might send it over the edge and then where would we be? If I had to do parent's evening by myself and then came home to a broken washing machine, I might just go on strike.

Shoving a load of whites into the machine and switching it on while the potatoes merrily boiled over in the kitchen, I warned the boys that they would be on hanging-out-the-wet-washing-in-the-conservatory duty after supper while I was up at the school. Surely they couldn't get into too much mischief doing that?

Hmmm! No comment.

23: Headway

Definition: moving forwards or making progress in spite of conditions which slow you down.

Let us return to the reconstruction project in the past again....

It came to pass that I was sat on my drive again, waiting for the arrival of more workmen. The chippies, (sadly that is short for the carpenters not the Chippendales!) were on their way to begin the next stage of our crumbly cottage reconstruction project.

Fortunately there was none of the nonsense that had marked my previous vigil for builders and the new team turned up on time with The Boss in attendance once again. I was a bit concerned at this latter development as I had learned the hard way that The Boss' appearances generally coincided with the news that there was a 'slight problem' which usually meant we needed to find more money. There wasn't any more money, we were up to our eyeballs and beyond in debt but I didn't think that was going to stop him. It wasn't his fault, I did realise that, but the job was a complicated one.

It turned out that I was right, unfortunately, and once he had introduced his new team and set them to work he asked if he might have a word in private. Deciding that I couldn't hear this without some form of sustenance, I invited him around to the kitchen and put the kettle on (yes, again!). Armed with a plate of cookies, I drifted over to the table and invited him to sit down and tell me what the problem was.

Apparently the issue was with the staircase. Previously we had been the proud owners of an extremely ancient set of rickety stairs that were full of charm and character, if not terribly safe or practical. As is often the way in old cottages, the original set of stairs had been constructed in a fairly ad-hoc manner and squeezed into a ridiculously small area which in no way conformed to modern building regulations. The new staircase would have to abide by the up-to-date rules. Today's conundrum was that a modern staircase would not fit where the old one had been.

There were two interconnecting issues associated with this situation. Firstly the current rules meant that each step on a staircase had to be even and regular, which is perfectly reasonable and completely unlike that which we had had before. I had no problem with this rule whatsoever. So many people had fallen down the old set of stairs over the years that a nice, new, safe set of treads sounded like a jolly good idea to me. The problem was going to be how to get a whole flight of them in to the area designated.

The second issue related to the ceiling height for the ground floor. Modern building regulations also had rules with regard to the minimum height (floor to ceiling) that was acceptable in a room; this figure definitely didn't match with how low our old ceilings used to be. Again I had no problem with this either. I was fed up with people banging their heads on low beams all the time. (Not that I had experienced a problem myself, having stopped growing at just over five foot, but people don't half grumble when they walk slap bang into stray chunks of wood innocently hanging around the place.)

Now on the whole this wasn't going to be a problem as we could steal the extra height out of the roof space. It would just mean a smaller loft and slightly more sloped ceilings upstairs. As I've mentioned, I don't do lofts, so I didn't care what size it was. (Unless smaller lofts mean smaller spiders of course, but I don't think it works like that.) Therefore ceiling height was only an issue when it came to the actual staircase.

Unfortunately, a higher ceiling downstairs translated into a need for a bigger staircase, and we were struggling to fit our original staircase length back in, so increasing the size would be a significant problem. We were going to have to pay extra (what a surprise) for a custom-made staircase which would make things a bit easier to fit on a practical level, but it would still need to have a set number of stairs at regular intervals within a certain distance to conform to the rules.

As The Boss and I were pouring over a plan of the ground floor considering our options, Logic stumbled sleepily in from the caravan to locate a late breakfast. The sixth form were on an inset day and she and her sister had been making full use of the extra revision time this afforded them by having a nice long lie in.

Having loaded the toaster and made a couple of cups of tea to take back out to the caravan on a tray when the toast was ready, she eventually came over to have a nose at what was occupying us at the table.

The phrase 'you can't see for looking' is quite true sometimes. We had been staring at the plans until we were going cross eyed, but once we had explained to Logic what our little enigma was, she immediately said "I assume you've tried the obvious haven't you?"

I should explain here that Logic is a puzzle freak. She loves spending hours doing impossible jigsaws, so she can usually see how things fit together very quickly. I don't mean the standard 1,000 piece jigsaws. I mean three dimensional ones, and the type that has an impossible and almost identical picture printed on *both* sides so that you don't know which side relates to which puzzle. I don't see how she does them. She can't see any difficulty.

She even likes constructing flat packed furniture too! A skill that would come in very handy when we eventually moved back in; after all we had half a house-worth of dismantled furniture piled up in the garage waiting for her.

Anyway, back to the staircase riddle.

Quite clearly Logic could tell from our blank expressions that we had no idea what she was talking about. At the same time, I could tell from her face that we had missed something pretty fundamental.

"Well, it is tricky, but..." there was a moment's pause before she sat down next to me and pulled a pencil from the knot of long dark hair she had piled loosely on top of her head.

"May I?" she asked politely whilst firmly sliding the plans out from under The Boss' reluctant fingers. For a minute or two she looked closely at the dimensions outlined and then started to quickly jot down a systematic series of numbers in the margin of the plan.

The Boss tried to object and pull his plans back across the table out of her reach, but she merely held on tighter, shushed him and carried on writing.

I watched both her actions and The Boss' reaction with amusement. I should probably explain that Logic is a gifted mathematician, and I had seen her enthralled by numbers many times before but The Boss had not and the alternating annoyed and suspicious looks he was casting her way were extremely entertaining. I could tell he wasn't terribly happy about this small, sleepy, seventeen year old girl scribbling all over his plans. He kept looking at me as if waiting for me to step in and tell her to stop but I merely raised my eyebrows in return and smiled serenely. It wasn't as if she was a toddler with a wax crayon. If there was a solution I was completely confident that Logic would find it.

Eventually her calculations ground to a halt and she replaced the pencil in her topknot and nudged the plans back towards him.

"There you go," she said with a yawn. "That'll give you the direction and angle, with the height, and length of the run including measurements for the sizes and regularity of the treads. I assume it'll be a custom-made job. If you use those figures then it'll fit!"

Fresh eyes on a conundrum always help, especially if they don't come with any pre-conceived ideas (and they belong to someone who is really good at maths, of course). We had been trying to fit the new staircase into the footprint of the old one. An impossible task in fact, but if you turned the whole thing ninety degrees and moved it over a bit towards the new porch then it worked. Easy!

It would mean that the entire layout of the inside of the property would have to be re-jigged on the plan but they hadn't started constructing it yet so that wouldn't be a problem. Logic had kindly included altered figures there too. The Boss looked at it for a long moment in silence before nodded briefly. "That does look as though it might work," he conceded reluctantly. "I'll just run that by the structural engineer to double check the numbers are correct, and then run off a new plan for building control."

He was so busy rolling up his plans that he didn't spot Logic raising a single eyebrow at me and me grimacing sympathetically back. Her numbers were always correct, I knew that from experience, but The Boss didn't. I subtly shook my head at her. We had to let the project leader do his job. He would find out soon enough that she was right.

"I'll let the boys know that the dimensions are probably changing. They'll need to order a staircase to the new figures once they've been confirmed and then we'll be off and running with the next stage," he said as he stood up. "They can build the porch roof for you while we are waiting for the finalised figures for the new internal layout. With any luck we'll have some electricians and plumbers on site too by the end of the week." With an emphatic tap of his rolled up plans on the table he turned and headed for the door.

***

It turned out that Logic was right (I told you so!) the staircase was going to fit in the new location and the re-jigged internal layout would work as well. The Boss was right too as we had both electricians and plumbers on site by the end of the week as well as the carpenters. As a result the construction related noise levels from the front of the house increased massively.

Over the course of the next week, now that the dinky digger had gone back from whence it came, Skelly resumed his supervisory role from his perch on the bench by the garage. The chippies weren't quite sure what to make of this and gave him quite a wide berth to begin with, but they soon relaxed and the work cracked on a pace. Beams went in, stud walls went up and wires and pipes were laid in all directions. It was quite staggering just how quickly the inside of the cottage was coming together. One morning in particular my phone was constantly going off at work. Each time it was a different question about light fittings, radiators and doorways etc. There was so much progress being made in such a short time. It was all positive and so very exciting but simultaneously exhausting.

Back at the house there was a continuous cacophony of sawing, shouting, and banging with the ever present radio playing in the back ground, but I didn't mind. The house was beginning to look like a house again. It was possible to start thinking that we might actually get to move back in properly and live a normal life, well, as normal as life ever gets with us.

Several days later, I was contentedly chopping up vegetables in the kitchen listening to the sounds of building work through the temporary stud wall between the kitchen and the front section of the house, when I heard one of the chippies say loudly, "Hang on a minute, where's Tiny gone?"

It took a moment to register what had been said, and just as I was starting to wonder what or who Tiny was, I heard the cat start to hiss and spit behind me! Turning towards the open patio doors I froze. There was the most enormous

Great Dane standing in the conservatory staring at me, with a long drool-covered bone sticking out either side of its jaws. He took a tentative step towards me and the cat shot off the flagstone floor and scrambled up my trouser leg, then my t-shirt to my shoulders where she hid under my hair and growled menacingly. The big toughie! I was actually quite impressed. She was getting on a bit now and I hadn't seen her move so fast for years. Unfortunately for me, my skin was now decorated with hundreds of little puncture marks as evidence of her newly rediscovered speed and agility.

The massive dog merely put its head on one side curiously and continued to drool.

Now I believe I have already mentioned the fact that we had a lot of extras living in the house with us at that time, in the form of spiders and mice, but I draw the line at letting random dogs just walk in too. (Been there, done that, bought the T-shirt!) If I did, I might as well invite the horses in from the field next door too and be done with trying to run a civilised household.

Standing stock still I raised my voice to carry through the wooden partition to the workmen and I said "I think you'll find that Tiny is round here!"

"Oh Heck!" (No, he actually said something much fruitier than that in reality.)"Hang on I'll be round in a sec!" came an anxious voice.

Within a minute Tiny was joined by an apologetic carpenter. A compact, wiry man who was covered, head to toe, in sawdust burst through the patio doors and tried to persuade Tiny to follow him out of the kitchen.

Tiny really didn't want to leave. He was eyeing my cowardly cat with extremely intense interest.

"I am so sorry," said Dusty. "He's only a puppy. My wife's gone away to look after her mother. I can't leave him at home alone. I thought he was asleep in the car but he must have woken up and gone for a wander. I'll try to keep him round the front if it's OK with you." He looked so worried that I had to smile.

"No harm done, I just wasn't expecting him, that's all," I said, attempting to carefully unpeel the reluctant cat from around my neck. "He's perfectly welcome outside, as long as he doesn't eat my cat, of course. She really wouldn't appreciate it. Can I suggest that it would probably be a good idea to keep him on a longish leash round the front though? Some of the cars that come along the lane are ever so fast. I'd hate for him to get squashed."

Dusty sighed with relief and nodded. "OK, thanks I will."

"One thing though," I said as he turned to go. "Do you think you could persuade him to give my skeleton back his leg please?

PART 6

"It is not in the stars to hold our destiny but in ourselves."

William Shakespeare

24: Exacting

Definition: making significant demands on one's skills resources and ability

Coming forward to the present day once again...

It was at least three days before I was able to return to my big dark green canvas and spend any time on it because, parents' evening aside, so much of life seemed to conspire to keep us apart. However, finally I made it into my studio, shut the door firmly behind me and then the paint literally started to fly. It was as if I had painted this so many times already in my head that my fingers knew what to do without being told. In fact that was exactly what had happened. Over the last three days the actions that I needed to take to complete this piece had been rehearsed over and over on a separate loop in my head whilst in reality I was getting on with going to work, doing the washing, the shopping and cooking dinners.

Several hours later I stepped back from the canvas utterly exhausted. It was finished. In the same way that the blackest of nights eventually ends with the glimmer of the new day dawning, so the bleakest of winters is beaten with the arrival of the first new shoots of spring. This latest painting was alive with new spring growth. Buttercups, bluebells and daisies all vied for space among deep green leaves on the canvas. Bright, energetic and colourful, it was a massively pivotal piece for me that I felt was indicative of just how much better I was getting.

I staggered out of my little studio and collapsed in an exhausted heap onto the sofa by the fireplace. Several minutes passed as I sat there not moving, and then the telephone rang. Fortunately it was on the coffee table right next to me, as no one ever remembers to put it back on the base to charge. I reached over and picked it up, certain that it would be one of those silent electronically generated cold calls. We get a lot of those. Only it wasn't. A very refined female voice was asking to speak to me.

I sat up a bit and confirmed that it was me answering the phone.

"Oh that's great!" the lady enthused, "I keep leaving messages for you, but I am sure you've been very busy."

I vaguely remembered Quiet giving me several messages that I hadn't really listened to in the last few days.

"Yes, sorry, I have." I agreed sheepishly.

"Oh don't worry about that," she said breezily. "I know what you creative types are like. Anyway I just wanted to let you know that I have a space coming up for a two week exhibition if you'd like it. It's not for a couple of months so there's no great panic but we've been let down by another artist who is taking her work to a big gallery in New York. While I am very excited for her, it means that I am looking for something fresh and new to fill the space and I think your work would fit the bill nicely. We'd need about twenty canvases, medium to large."

"Um, how do you know my work is what you want?" I asked feeling like I was missing something fairly vital. My foggy brain was struggling to keep up. As far as I was aware she hadn't seen any of my paintings.

"Well I'm looking at the jpegs your agent sent through on my laptop now. I particularly like the fish, very positive and motivating, especially the message behind it; the whole looking up from the depths of the ocean and moving towards the light. Your agent tells me there is an art therapy story behind the work which sounds interesting too. And everyone likes fish," she said.

'Quiet doesn't' I mentally muttered to myself but at the same time I was also thinking 'What agent?'

"I like the feathers too. I think they will prove very popular. So spiritual. People have a thing about Guardian Angels don't they."

The jpeg comment helped some pieces of the puzzle to slot into place. I remembered the weekend that Chaos and Logic had both come back from university together. This must be what Chaos had been plotting when I had caught her taking photos in my studio. She never actually said what she wanted the photos for but she was quite capable of sending jpegs out to galleries without me knowing about it. She'd also make a pretty good agent, come to think of it. I wondered vaguely who else she'd contacted.

"Really?" I said faintly, "My agent, how very enterprising of her."

If I remembered correctly this lady was from a prominent gallery in the nearby town. It wasn't the usual sort of run-of-the-mill pretentious place that was stuffed with weird creations, but a gorgeous old building housing genuinely beautiful and uniquely stunning, artwork. The owner had an excellent reputation locally for promoting home grown artists and was a successful artist herself, having exhibited all over the world. She also ran all sorts of inspiring workshops to encourage people to try creative art-related activities themselves. Exhibitions in these sorts of places don't get handed out to just anyone. I'm not sure I would ever have had the courage to approach her. Not that such a thing would ever stop Chaos. This was quite an opportunity.

"Yes she's really keen on your work. She says you have quite a few completed canvasses available."

"That's true," I admitted, thinking of the huge stacks lurking in random locations around the house and garden.

"Well that all sounds very promising. Tell you what, I'll pencil you in for those two weeks and perhaps I can pop over sometime next week and take a look in person. Does that sound OK?"

I paused and then said, "Yes, alright. You do that." I didn't see what choice I had. Even though exhibitions are very draining, and require massive amounts of hard work it seemed that I was going to be doing this one.

I am pretty certain that Chaos would kill me if I didn't.

25: Emergent

Definition: in the process of developing or coming into existence.

Back in the past...

Now that Thor had left the site, we weren't quite so inundated by love-struck teenagers hoping to catch a glimpse of him with his top off. Nevertheless, the repair job was moving on at a cracking pace and we still had a reasonably high turnover of adolescent visitors. The dreaded A level and AS level exams were looming ever more closely so the amount of revision needed was getting pretty serious and they all needed to concentrate. As a result the level of noise from the communal study sessions on the patio was significantly less these days. However I wasn't used to complete silence.

My well-oiled parenting radar is still going strong after all these years and I have learned to my cost that silence nearly always means trouble. So you can understand my concern when I realised that there was absolutely no chatting what so ever coming from the teens one afternoon. There wasn't even the distant echo of the two boy Barbarians tackling each other to the ground for possession of some form of inflated, roughly spherical bag of wind.

Creeping over to the conservatory I could see that my random collection of students were all stood staring out over the grass and concentrating intently. They all seemed completely mesmerised, apart from Logic who was attempting to use her British Sign Language skills to signal something to me from behind her back whilst she looked out into the garden at the same time. I couldn't really understand her, but it looked a bit like she was trying to say 'come over here, slowly and quietly'. So I did.

I tiptoed up behind her and stared over her shoulder into the garden. "What are we looking at?" I murmured, after a minute had passed and I couldn't see anything of interest. Perhaps they had all gone a bit mad. Too much studying in all this beautiful sunshine can do that.

"Look!" she whispered, pointing very slowly, "under the caravan." I followed the direction of her finger and was immediately transfixed by the sight of a small round bundle of fluff peeping out from behind the caravan steps. Thank heavens I had my glasses on or I would never have spotted it.

As I watched, another one appeared, and then another.

My goodness!

It would seem that Hattie (that's what the Barbarians had named the caravan) had been sheltering more than just us in recent months. I had been congratulating myself that the inside of the caravan was a wildlife-free zone, but obviously underneath it was a different matter entirely. An expectant, wild rabbit, probably from the warren two fields over, had decided to make a nest for her babies under our caravan. This was a bizarre decision to my mind, given the noise we must have been making and the associated activity on our building site house, but it is quite common for them to do something like this apparently. An excellent example of hiding in plain sight with the theory being that a predator (like a fox) would be less likely to venture near to the caravan so the nest would be safer.

Quite clearly the mother rabbit's logic had been correct but I really hoped that Dusty was genuinely keeping the delightful Tiny on a lead now. It would be a shame to traumatise all these spellbound students by letting them watch a 'puppy' massacre these sweet, little bouncing baby bunnies as they were enjoying their first outing in the sunshine.

Eventually the mother rabbit put in an appearance, after we had counted at least six cute, little bundles of brown fluff, and started to marshal them off out of the garden and towards the nearby warren.

The students gave a heartfelt group sigh as the little cotton tails disappeared from sight and then immediately fell to chattering about how cute they were. I took this as my cue to disappear back into the kitchen. It was getting late in the afternoon and there was no way I was going to be able to shake off any of the additional teenagers without feeding them first. I figured that half a dozen pizzas were probably in order and set about making up the dough for them and chopping up a selection of toppings.

***

A short while later, with the oven stuffed to the brim with bread, tomato sauce, ham and melting cheese, I left Chaos and Logic loading up the next batch of pizzas with toppings, while I filled a tray with fresh cups of tea and took a brief trip around to see how the builders were getting on.

On the way, I trotted past Skelly who was reading a copy of The Financial Times. I observed with interest that his femur had been fully restored and that Tiny had taken up residence at his feet. The huge dog was apparently asleep in the sunshine, but I couldn't help notice that he occasionally stuck out his enormous tongue and gave the skeleton's lower leg a quick lick when he thought no one was looking. I made a mental note to check that Skelly had all his associated parts later that evening after Tiny had gone home.

The chippies were looking very pleased with themselves when I stepped through the gap in the wall that was the front porch entrance, and so they should be. The inside of the cottage was really taking shape. Dusty enthusiastically invited me to inspect all the work they had done that day which involved using a ladder (still no staircase yet) and admiring the upstairs rooms. The team were proudly showing off the new layout complete with ceilings, floor and doors that they failed to spot that I was totally terrified about how on earth I was going to get back down to ground level again. Ladders and I do not have a good relationship. Up is OK, but down?...... Not so much! Thank goodness I was wearing trousers not a skirt otherwise things could have got rather undignified.

It was a bizarre feeling to be able to walk around upstairs again after over ten months, but lovely at the same time to see that the children's bedrooms were starting to take shape if only as a very basic framework. I could really see how our home was slowly being restored to us which made me feel quite emotional.

Nevertheless, Dusty was keen to discuss a few technical issues with me that might hold proceedings up. There's always something isn't there?

Apparently the main problem of the moment was with the upstairs windows. Due to the fact that we had raised the ceiling heights downstairs, the windows on the first floor were going to be quite low down in proportion to the floor, with the windowsills approximately at knee height. They couldn't be moved up as the windows needed to be able to open outwards beneath the overhang of the beautiful original thatched roof. That wasn't a problem in my mind as the low windows looked completely in keeping with the whole slightly quirky, rustic cottage ambiance.

Unfortunately the health and safety elf didn't agree. It would seem that we had to have bars on these low windows to stop us accidentally throwing ourselves out of them. The rebuild would not be able to be signed off by building control otherwise.

However in contrast to this directive, the fire department were saying that we were not allowed to have bars on the windows in case there was a fire and we actually did want to throw ourselves out deliberately in order to escape the flames and couldn't. So we were rather caught between two different completely contradictory aspects of the health and safety system.

Dusty fortunately had a plan to get round this by designing some removable bars for the windows which would hopefully mean we could comply with both requirements. As he was enthusiastically explaining his ingenious invention in the minutest of exhaustive details I could feel my attention beginning to wander.

Casting an eye towards the door to the bedroom that had been sealed up so many months ago I was pleased to see that the tape around the insulating board looked like it was still holding. Hopefully it would keep out all the dust from the construction work for a little bit longer. I wondered how the little girl on the swing had fared through the cold, wet of the winter. It wouldn't be very much longer before we could open the partition up and find out.

Eventually Dusty ground to a halt and looked expectantly at me. Having not heard a word he'd said in at least the last five minutes I smiled and nodded at him and said "I think that sounds ingenious. Well done!" Which was obviously the right response as he grinned, looking very pleased with himself.

With a lot of well-meant, but not very practical, encouragement from the carpentry team, I successfully made it back down the ladder without disgracing myself and returned to the kitchen, just in time to rescue the second batch of pizzas from the oven before they burned. Only a few moments after that I was ferrying them out to the teenagers on the patio who fell on them ravenously as if they hadn't demolished four already. It looked like we were going to be requiring considerably more pizza at this rate!

26: Culmination

Definition: to start to bring something to a close or to reach a climactic point.

Remaining in the past....

As with many building projects, things can seem to take forever before one sees any progress and then all of a sudden everything starts to come together. This is the stage that we were now at with the rebuild of our beautiful cottage.

At long last the new staircase went in, the walls were plastered and the space started to feel almost useable again, instead of some noisy old barn stuffed to the brim with busy builders. I took such great delight in walking up and down the brand new, modern, safe set of stairs that I think poor old Dusty thought I had finally lost the plot. I was so pleased with it that I even went to get the Barbarians from the caravan to come and try it out too.

The Barbarians completely understood my fascination with the new stairs. We had spent so many years with the old rickety 350 year old cottage staircase that it was a complete novelty to have a full set of even, steady treads complete with a handrail! Fancy that!! Marvellous! All five of us spend a merry half an hour testing the new flight out and then going into each of the newly rebuilt bedrooms and generally getting in the way of the bemused workforce. Then I took lots of photos of the four Barbarians on the stairs with Skelly and sent the images to Beloved Husband at work to cheer him up.

Eventually, having been physically prevented from trying to get poor Skelly to slide down the new, unpainted bannister, Small changed the subject and nodded towards the sealed up back bedroom door saying bluntly, “So when are you going to open that up then?” He was only trying to distract me. I knew he’d already made his mind up to try the banister sliding thing later when I wasn’t looking, but I had to agree that he had a point about the little bedroom.

The bulk of the really dusty work had been completed. The carpentry, the plastering and the electrics were almost finished bar a few minor details. We even had a front door! Amazing! A beautiful forest green one with a little glass window in it and sleek, black fittings. We were now able to actually secure our property after nearly fourteen months with a gaping hole in the wall direct to the outside world. Wonders would never cease. Such a small detail but so important to a family’s sense of security and one that signalled that yet another significant change was on its way.

It really wouldn’t be long before we could start to move back into the house and begin to live like normal people do once more. It all needed painting and then carpets of course, but that would not take long. The funny thing was that we were all getting a bit nervous about it. Had you told us last year that we’d get twitchy about moving back in, I would have told you not to be so daft; but now that the time was approaching none of us felt ready. Maybe it had something to do with not trusting the house not to fall down again – I simply don’t know! To distract myself, I had been focussing on mentally organising all the various jobs that would need to be done to achieve complete resettlement in our home, but it seemed that the Barbarians had other more fundamental issues on their minds.

Quiet was standing in the door way to his new/old bedroom. It was a new door in a slightly different place to the old one due to the altered staircase layout, but the room was generally where his old bedroom used to be, it was just a different shape to how it was before. He had a pensive expression on his face.

“What’s wrong?” I asked.

There was a pause before he answered doubtfully, “It’s a bit big, isn’t it?”

“Yeah!” said Logic uncertainly, “Mine is too! What on earth are we supposed to do with all this space?”

I looked at them both in total surprise. Were they joking?

It would seem not. They both had genuinely perturbed looks on their faces. This was not a reaction that I had expected.

It should be born in mind that cob walls tend to be at least three foot deep. In contrast, modern walls are nowhere near that thick, so they were quite correct that both bedrooms were significantly bigger than they had been before even though the external dimensions of the house hadn’t changed.

I had thought they would be delighted but they had been living an existence of complete uncertainty, in a very confined space, for such a long period of time. They had spent over a year with next to no elbow room. Their accommodation in the caravan was extremely snug and they had all coped incredibly well with being crammed into such a small area, their personal belongings thinned down to the absolute bare minimum. This new change, even though it was what we had all been working towards for so long, was obviously going to take some adapting to.

“I am sure you’ll get used to it!” I said encouragingly. “We can’t move back in just yet, but when we can, you should take your time. Remember, it’ll look far more like home with paint on the walls, some curtains and carpets. Maybe try it out for a night or two and see how you feel. We won’t be able to remove the caravan terribly quickly anyway so there’ll still be space outside if you prefer to stay there for a bit. We’ll need time to put together all your furniture again and then you’ll be able to get all your clothes and books and other things out of the boxes in the sheds, which will be nice.”

Quiet nodded and shrugged. Logic chewed on the inside of her cheek and stayed silent.

“I can’t wait!” said Chaos cheerfully. It was nice to know her enthusiasm for throwing herself headfirst into things without looking too carefully hadn’t been dimmed by events. There’s a lot to be said for not overthinking things. “Now, answer the question, when are you going to open up that room?”

“Well!” I said, “I guess there’s no time like the present!”

Dusty, who was probably desperate to get us out of the new bedrooms so he and the electricians could finish up for the afternoon, handed me a Stanley knife and I stepped up to the sealed-off door. Running the knife blade through the tape I cut the plastic sheeting and insulation board free from the door frame and eased them out of the gap. Quiet lifted them from me as if they weighed nothing and then passed them back to the builders.

Reaching for the handle I turned it slowly and opened the door. Light flooded the room from the open curtains and lit up thousands of little dust motes suspended in the air above all the boxes and furniture that filled the space. Across the packed room I met the eyes of the little girl on the swing.

She seemed pleased to see me.

The Barbarians crowded into the small space behind me, silently looking around the once familiar room. It was a very surreal experience seeing all these old belongings in what was effectively a time capsule of our lives before the collapse. We probably could have stood there for ages just looking but Dusty was keen to move things along and called through the doorway, "Do you want us to take the temporary partition downstairs apart now too, so you can come through from the kitchen? Then you won't have to walk all the way round the outside anymore to bring us tea."

"Oh!" I exclaimed, "Is it time to do that already?"

"I don't see why not!" he said. "Now the porch is finished and the front door is on, everything is secure. There's no real need to keep the front and back separated off. I've got a set of front door keys for you downstairs too." The thought of having a door key again was really quite exciting. I hadn't realised how much I had missed having an operational front door, let alone a key. How civilised!

The boys had perked up at the idea of watching the partition coming down. They were no doubt envisaging sledge hammers and other destructive action, but I rather thought that they would be disappointed as Thor wasn't here anymore. Dusty was significantly more cautious in nature and likely to take very good care of the new plasterwork nearby.

"Sure, OK!" I agreed, quickly leaning over the piles of boxes and reaching to lift down the little painting before turning to follow everyone else down the stairs. Our house was about to start becoming a functioning home again.

Dismantling the partition really wasn't that exciting, but it was a massively significant moment nonetheless. Beloved Husband made it home from work just as the initial sections of hardboard were being removed and he and the Barbarians thoroughly enjoyed walking through the archway several times just for the sheer novelty of it, after Dusty had finished. Yet more photos had to be taken and dispatched onto social media to prove that we had a whole house again; then we decided that a celebratory piece of cake and a round of hot chocolates in the kitchen was a fitting way to mark the occasions.

I carefully wrapped the half-painted little girl in bubble wrap and tucked her away safely before joining the rest of the family.

27: Perseverance

Definition: steadfast determination to achieve something regardless of obstacles in the way.

Now for some positive progress in the present....

Having committed myself to meeting with the Gallery owner the next week I went into my studio and started to think about what this might actually mean.

The bubble wrapped package on the window sill next to the radio caught my eye. Then I held out my right hand and watched it carefully for several minutes observing the tremor. It was definitely less pronounced than it had been. Perhaps it was time for this one last challenge. Picking up the parcel I started to break the seal.

Unwrapping it quickly I stared at the small, half-finished canvas as the plastic bubbles fell to the floor. The little girl on the swing had waited a very long time for me to get back to her, yet here she was as bright and cheerful as the day I had liberated her from her incarceration.

At that point in time, the day we regained our whole house back again, I hadn't ever planned on painting again. I probably would have destroyed this unfinished work then and there, had I not promised Beloved Husband that I would never again burn my work as I had done after the cottage initially collapsed. That awful destruction had come about as a result of our need to find sufficient space to accommodate the Barbarians more comfortably and to store all essential items that had been rescue from the disintegrating house, but it had also been a personal punishment. One I had inflicted on myself due to my feelings of guilt and helplessness at not being able to protect my children from what was happening.

In some respects Beloved Husband had been more distressed than I at the sight of all my paintings burning. Not because he liked the paintings particularly, although he didn't have anything against them either, but more due to his concern that I would regret my destructive impulse. My determination never to paint again had been unsustainable and he had known that I would eventually need to return to what I loved.

He was right I had missed my work. Not all of it. Some of the burned canvases were utter rubbish, but some good pieces had been lost as well and I did miss them. I wish things could have been different. But that sort of thinking doesn't get us anywhere does it?

So in order to keep Beloved Husband happy this little half completed painting didn't end up in the bin or on the bonfire, but had been hiding away, wrapped carefully in bubble wrap and tucked in the box of painting paraphernalia that I had then stored for a very long time at the back of my brand new under-stairs cupboard in our beautifully restored home. This retrieved canvas was small, about the size of an A4 piece of paper and easily tucked out of sight where I could pretend she didn't exist. Even when I had eventually started to paint again, I had never dared to unwrap her, until now.

I had been too afraid that there would never come a time when I would be able to finish her. I had known that I was damaged and that successfully completing this particular piece of work would only be possible if I actually managed to finally heal myself both mentally and physically. In my mind she had been a half-acknowledged goal to aim for in my attempts to put the pieces of my heart and soul back together.

I wondered if maybe it was now time to try finishing her.

There were a number of problems that this particular challenge presented me with, in addition to my dubious dexterity difficulties.

The fact of the matter was that it was well over three years since I had started this painting. At the time that I had been interrupted by the house falling down so long ago, I had had every intention of returning within hours, or a day at the most, to finish her but events had taken over and more pressing matters had resulted in her being abandoned.

Back then I had been working in traditional oils, using a wet in wet method. Traditional oils take quite a long time to dry, and in this case the (now completely dry) paint was quite thick in places. Both of these factors would mean that as she was completely dry, restarting the painting process was going to raise some problems. Any fresh work was going to have to be done very carefully so that there would be no future cracks developing between the old paint and the new.

It would no doubt be easier to simply start again on a fresh canvas but, to me, completing this little girl represented my journey as I came full circle from the artist I used to be to the artist I was now. She was important. I might never attempt a piece of work like this one ever again, but to my mind, finishing this painting would be like putting a triumphant full stop at the end of the tragic tale of the house that sat down. So I was determined to do it.

Arming myself with a selection of brushes and a jar of linseed oil, I sat down to rummage through my box of oil paints, picking out the exact same tubes I had used before. Setting the little canvas on the easel before me I reached over to flick the radio on and set to work.

28: Realisation

Definition: The achievement of something long awaited.

Finally, the day dawns in the past when we can move back in....

In spite of the incredible progress and the fact that we now had a functioning house, it took a while for us to get used to this new development. It felt really strange walking from back to front and vice versa without heading outside first.

There were still a million tiny things that needed to be done in order for us to be able to start moving back in and resume anything remotely resembling a normal life in a normal house.

Firstly we needed carpets before we could practically start re-populating the bedrooms. We didn't want to move all the furniture back in and then have to move it all out again so the carpets could be fitted, but there was a minor problem as usual. The carpets had been measured and ordered and delivered to the shop, but no one had thought to book a fitting date. Oops! So near and yet so far! There was a very long waiting list for carpet fitters apparently and we were at the back of it. It would seem that we might have to stay in the caravan for another couple of months which was very frustrating.

Just as we adjusted to this idea, there was a phone call out of the blue from the carpet company, telling us that there had been a cancellation and the fitters could potentially come the next day which was fantastic news but we hadn't yet finished painting the walls because we thought we would have more time. Beloved Husband accepted the booking for the next day. After he had hung up the handset he looked at me and said, “OK! We have 5 rooms and a double height hallway, walls ceiling and woodwork to paint in less than twenty four hours. Are you up for the challenge?” Just as I was about to firmly tell him I could do anything he could do, there was a muffled knock on the door. (‘Need to get a door knocker’ immediately went on my ‘to do’ list.)

Opening our lovely new front door, we were confronted by the Godfather. Not Robert De Niro, the real one. The Barbarians’ Godfather was standing on the drive and smiling broadly at us as he said “I’ve got the day off. Need a hand with anything?”

On closer inspection we noted that he was wearing well used painting overalls and carried a bag, out of which were sticking several paint brush handles. A most timely intervention! He probably wasn’t expecting to have to help us complete quite such a big job in quite such a short timescale but he didn’t complain, just got stuck in beside us. The Barbarians pitched in too when they got home from school and by the next morning, totally exhausted and covered in paint from head to toe, we opened the front door again to welcome the carpet fitters.

Carpets aside, there were a few snagging issues to sort out but considering the size of the job, not many. I did have to spend quite some time persuading our lovely, but rather OCD, electrician that I didn’t mind that the socket heights in all the rooms weren’t quite the same. I hadn’t even noticed that they were fractionally out to be honest, but he had and he wasn’t happy about it. Apparently one of his colleagues had done the measuring and hadn't been precise enough. I was just glad to have sockets.

It was only by spinning some nonsense about how I felt it was important for there to be some rustic variation so that the long sense of history of the house was preserved that I managed to persuade him not to rip them all out and start again. That would have put us back weeks and no doubt cost even more to fix, so I was relieved when I finally managed to convince him that sleepy, stressed out mothers in recently rebuilt cottages could cope with mismatching socket heights.

Once the painting and carpets, final electrical work and other snags were completed it was time to start sorting out what furniture was to be brought back into which rooms. So lengthy debates with regard to which legs went with which table and which doors went on which wardrobe etcetera began.

Eventually after what felt like a hellish week of constantly putting together flat pack furniture, without the assistance of the usual unhelpful instructions, definitely not the right pieces and apparently none of the correct screws (Even though I had been so careful to keep them all together in little bags and taped them to part of what they came from.) we finally managed to reassemble most of the bedroom furniture.

At last we could spend our first night back in our newly rebuilt home.

29: Apotheosis

Definition: The top most point in the development of something.

Now we have the final act in the present...

I couldn't believe just how busy the room was for the opening of the exhibition. Everywhere I looked I could see people mingling, drinking glasses of wine and chatting. Somewhere off to my left came the repetitive flash from a photographer who was recording the event for the local papers. Now, I hate crowded rooms at the best of time and I particularly hate having my photograph taken, so these circumstances would normally have me running for the hills. However this time I couldn't because all of these people were here for me, including the photographer. Not actually me specifically of course but my paintings and as the featured artist I had been told in no uncertain terms by the Gallery Owner that I needed to be here to generally mingle and network.

Fortunately the regular exercise sessions I had recently indulged in had not only improved my general fitness but also trimmed my figure down significantly, which gave me far more confidence than usual. The outfit I was wearing was my favourite. It had been consigned to the back of the wardrobe ages ago due to the fact that it had become far too snug. Not so anymore! I was definitely all on the inside of this gorgeous dress now and feeling pretty amazing with it.

Interestingly enough I hadn't had any episodes of palpitations in recent weeks either, so I was really beginning to feel very much better, no doubt a direct result of my new regime of self-care. Sharing regular, nutritious meals with Beloved Husband and our boys was something I looked forward to now, without constantly dwelling on the absent members of the family. I had come to terms with the sale of the house and no longer feared that moving would tear the family apart. As a direct consequence of that I no longer had that deep gnawing emptiness inside me. I still missed our girls, but wasn't obsessed about it anymore. They had bright futures ahead and I was so very proud of them.

I was adapting, morphing into a stronger, better me. The aching hollows in my heart, that I had been attempting to pack with junk food in a subconscious and futile attempt to fill them in, were now healing properly. Like our beautiful, restored cottage I was beginning to feel whole again for the first time since the old walls had crumbled.

On a lighter note, I also found, to my delight, that I was now able to occasionally treat myself to a cup of real tea or coffee, and the occasional glass of wine, as long as I didn't overdo it. Added to that, a good friend of mine (who also happens to be the most talented hairdresser on the planet, in my opinion) had kindly done something magical to my hair, blending colours and adding subtle highlights so that my grey streak now looked like a deliberate, quirky fashion statement. Therefore, if there had to be a photographer around for this event, at least I knew I had managed to scrub up relatively ok.

The last few weeks had flown by on a tidal wave of finalising all the necessary details for the gallery exhibition. Making sure I had sufficient pieces of the right dimensions to work together on the beautifully smooth white walls. Then ensuring all of the paintings were suitably framed, had the correct hanging attachments and were marked up and catalogued with the titles, descriptions and prices. After that came the on-line marketing and advertising campaign to bring in this crowd of interested people for the opening night. The crowd that were making me increasingly nervous, although when I looked closer I spotted several of my new friends from the WI and a few of the chaps from the taekwondo class, all chatting happily with each other while checking out my paintings.

"Stop looking at the door dear, I'm not going to let you run away you know!" said my glamorous new friend the Gallery Owner. She was a tall, slim striking woman dressed in a chic, black, layered ensemble with the most impressively high heeled zebra print statement shoes. I had no idea how she was managing to walk in them but she seemed perfectly poised and in complete control. I had liked her from the moment I met her when she came to the cottage to see my canvases. An artist herself, she was an incredibly knowledgeable, inspiring and energetic person. She had immediately insisted I double my prices and suggested that I introduce a line of cards and framed prints for the gallery in addition to the original canvases to be exhibited.

"You need to be here for this," she continued. "As I predicted, it is a tremendous success! Well done! Have you seen how many have sold already? We've only been open an hour and quite a few have already been reserved. I told you those feathers of yours would fly off the walls, not to mention the colourful animal paintings."

I had never intended to display many of these pieces, especially as some of the earlier ones had been fuelled by some very deep and painful emotions. Nevertheless now I could see the entire collection exhibited together they depicted a spectacular journey out of the darkness and into the light, especially when seen in the context of the very human story behind the work.

In a unique addition to the opening evening the Gallery Owner had persuaded me to give a short presentation to introduce my paintings and tell a little bit about the events behind their creation. I was terrified of standing up in front of all these people but if I could survive my house falling down then I wasn't going to let something like this beat me.

"It's OK," I answered, smiling "I'm not trying to escape, honestly. I'm just looking for my husband and my boys. They said they would be here....Ah" I trailed off in relief as the door opened at that point and in walked Beloved Husband and the boy Barbarians looking very smart indeed.

"They are here!" I explained and then exclaimed "Oh!"

Behind the boys I spotted Chaos and Logic looking extremely elegant as they made their way through the throng towards me.

"I didn't know you were coming!" I exclaimed in delight, giving each of the girls a gentle but heartfelt hug, taking great care not to rumple their gorgeous outfits. Of course I wouldn't dream of hugging the boys in public, their street cred wouldn't stand for it, so I just smiled and settled for patting them each, briefly, on the arm in welcome. All six of us together again! How wonderful!

“Sorry we’re late,” said Beloved Husband grabbing two glasses of sparkling wine from a passing waiter and handing me one. “Their train was late, but we made it in the end. You must have thought we weren’t coming. The girls made me promise not to tell you they were planning to be here. They wanted to surprise you.”

“Well they certainly did that!” I said, still grinning like a Cheshire cat. “I am so glad you’re here.” I took his free hand and squeezed it, looking into his beautiful blue eyes for a moment. “Thank you,” I said quietly, just for him.

He winked at me. “Anytime!”

“If you think your agent was going to miss this then you’ve got another think coming!” Chaos said sternly, but with a broad smile on her face.

“Yes!” I exclaimed, turning towards her again, “about that…”

“You know you’d never have got around to it,” interrupted Logic, grinning at her sister. “In fact I rather think you owe her one! Me too, for distracting you with cake so she could take the photos.”

By then, Small had completed a quick circuit of the room and briefly examined each of the canvases on the wall before coming back having blatantly pilfered an entire bowl of ‘posh’ crisps from the elegant buffet table at the end of the room.

“What do the red dots mean?” he piped up from around a crunchy mouthful.

"When someone wants to buy a painting, the gallery put a red dot on the information card on the wall next to it to show that the original is no longer available for sale to anyone else. Then when the exhibition is over the painting can be taken away."

"So you've sold some then!" he said triumphantly.

"Actually I have!" I said with a grin looking pointedly at Quiet, "You won't believe this but quite a few of the guardian angel paintings have gone and several of the fish ones too."

"There's no accounting for taste," he said solemnly before flashing me a quick sideways grin.

"No!" I agreed, smiling back at him. "There isn't is there?"

"Right!" said Logic, tucking one of her arms through mine and one through Chaos'. "Let's have a look round at these paintings then. It's so nice to see them on display and not just chucked in the shed. Come on!" Leaving the boys to raid the food supplies, we set of on a tour of the room together. The girls exclaimed over how well the canvases looked in the space with all the sophisticated lighting. Eventually we made it to what I felt was the most important painting, the centrepiece of the whole exhibition, the small canvas of a little girl on a swing.

"You finished her!" said Chaos.

"Yes I did. It took me long enough!"

"She's beautiful!" said Logic. "Well done!"

The rest of the open evening passed in a happy blur. Now that I had my rocks around me to steady my nerves I could deal with the crowds of people and even enjoy circulating and chatting with everyone.

It was really interesting to hear the various discussions on the paintings too. Especially the comments that arose about the fully dressed skeleton reading a tabloid newspaper, sitting on a wrought iron bench in the corner of the gallery sporting a complete builder's outfit including hard hat, reinforced, muddy boots, concrete encrusted trousers, a faded flannel shirt and luminous waistcoat (all cast offs kindly donated by our fabulous building team when they left us).

Anything goes in art apparently and while I had merely not wanted to leave Skelly out on my big night, most of the guests seemed to think that he was actually a deliberate and very thought provoking 'installation' piece. People were even sitting next to him on the bench and taking selfies. He was so popular in fact that the boys had to put their own red dot next to him to make sure that he wasn't accidentally sold.

In a brief lull later on I dared to ask the girls how long they were back for.

"I've got to go back for my results next week and then I will be home for the summer," said Chaos.

"Really? That's wonderful news," I said trying to contain my delight.

"Yeah!" said Logic, "University is great fun. I've enjoyed every minute of it and I am looking forward to going back next year, but you're stuck with me from now until September, because I've already finished. I got my old job back in town for the summer, starting Monday."

"You should see how much washing she's brought back," teased Chaos. "It's all in the back of Dad's car."

"Oh great!" I exclaimed and rolled my eyes, pretending exasperation, "my poor washing machine!" Leaning over I gave Logic a quick hug. "Only joking! Welcome back!"It seemed that my fears that my babies would not want to come back to live with their parents, who had been so stressed and anxious and who were now selling their childhood home, were totally unfounded. They might only be here for the summer but it didn't matter. They had chosen to come back to us and that was what was most important.

Beloved Husband slung his arm around my shoulders and gave me a squeeze. The boys trailed after him, each with a large plate of food in hand. "Happy now?" he asked.

"Oh yes!" I said beaming broadly at everyone and thinking how lucky I was to have these amazing people in my life!

"Really happy!"

Epilogue – the final word from the author.

There, my dear friends, is an appropriate place to draw an end to my tale.

Our heroine is once again surrounded by those she loves; the people who have helped her to stick the broken parts of herself back together. She is wrapped in the warm, double embrace of both their unfailing support and the unexpected success of her work; the many paintings that have been such a key part of her recovery as she climbed slowly and steadily out of the terrifying abyss of complete mental and physical exhaustion.

I think it is possible to spend far too long searching for meaning in events. One can frequently hear people saying that things occur for a reason. Often they do, but I believe that sometimes things just happen and then it is essential to focus on simply surviving. Afterwards, as the phoenix rises from the ashes, it is possible to emerge stronger and (hopefully) wiser than before.

With her Beloved Husband and the adored Barbarian Horde around her our heroine is going to be absolutely fine; and so we'll leave her now with her bright, creative future in front of her as she uses her newly forged strength to move on from the disasters of the past.

I wonder what she will get up to next. We'll just have to wait and see.... ☺ x

Restoration

Definition: the process or act of returning something to its previous condition, to rebuild or repair.

More paintings by Alice May can be seen on the website.
www.alicemay.weebly.com
or you can watch Alice May paint on YouTube by searching for 'alice may artist author'

The End

for now...

Restoration

The Helpful Hippy
Caffeine-free alternatives to tea and coffee.

Once the Helpful Hippy started to educate me on caffeine-free drinks I was amazed at the sheer number of alternatives to tea and coffee which are available.

I include a very simple list here with the recommendation that if you are seriously interested in reducing your caffeine intake then it is worth doing a bit of personal research before you start. After all there is a lot of information on the internet promising major wide reaching health benefits of these alternatives but I can't tell what is actually advertising and what is genuinely accurate so it's best if you make up your own mind.

I'm a bit of a cynic really (unlike the helpful hippy)!

Rooibos or Red Bush Tea - Herbal infusions from the South African Red Bush.

Roasted Grains - A variety of Korean and/or Japanese teas made from barley, corn, or brown rice.

White Coffee - A soothing tisane made from orange blossom water. I have to admit I haven't tried this but it sounds amazing!

Hot Ginger, Honey and Lemon - This is reportedly popular for its medicinal qualities, and is very soothing if you are under the weather, but I have to confess I like adding a dash of whiskey as it is so like the hot toddies my grandmother used to make. (Not that I am recommending you do such a thing of course!)

Herbal Teas
My personal favourite is the blackcurrant and vanilla herbal tea from Lidl with the tea bag left in the cup as the water cools down. Delicious!!

Chaos and Logic's 'slightly lower sugar' sweet treats

Realising that their mother stood no chance of successfully 'treating her body like a temple' as suggested by the Helpful Hippy down the hall, Chaos and Logic perfected a few lower sugar recipes so that she could still have a treat while she got better. After all, the doctor recommended she reduce her refined sugar intake, not avoid sweet things entirely.

Please note that these are not recipes that are intended to be used for weight loss in any way, or for any medical reason, so please don't do so. They are merely recipes which switch out some of the refined sugar for a more natural alternative. My girl Barbarians refuse to use artificial sweeteners in their baking (something that the Helpful Hippy whole-heartedly agrees with).

As these taste great and I'd like them to keep baking them for me, I agree with them too.

Honey Shortbread

Preheat the oven to 150°C, 300°F, or gas mark 2.
Layer a loose sheet of grease-proof paper on top of a baking tray.

Ingredients:
110g (4oz) butter
50g (2oz) honey (or maple syrup depending on your budget and preference)
175g (6oz) plain flour
Optional 25g (1oz) dried chopped fruit of your choice.

Shove all the ingredients, apart from the fruit, into the whizzy doofer (a.k.a. Magimix or equivalent whizzy device) and blitz them together until they form a paste. Tip the paste out onto a clean work surface and fold in the dried fruit. Press into a ball before rolling out into a fat sausage shape.

Using a sharp knife slice sections off the fat sausage shape and lie flat on the baking sheet/tray. (You could dust these lightly in brown sugar if you really need to, just don't tell the helpful hippy!)

Bake in the centre of the oven for 30 minutes, then take out and cool on a wire rack if you can.

Personally, I am surprised these shortbread biscuits even make it as far as the oven because the uncooked honey shortbread mix is lovely. Those that do manage to get cooked don't usually survive the cooling down stage as Quiet and Small are known to inhale them before they hit the cooling rack (assuming their mother doesn't get there first of course).

Beware, a polite queue can often be seen forming near the oven when these biscuits are baking. We are British after all!

Honey, Chocolate and Orange Drizzle Cake

Preheat the oven to 170°C, 325°F, or gas mark 3.
Line a 1lb loaf tin with grease-proof paper.

Ingredients:
For the cake:
110g (4oz) self-raising flour

1tsp baking powder
110g (4oz) butter
60g dark brown sugar
50g (2 tablespoons) honey
1 tablespoon cocoa powder
2 large eggs

For the icing
The juice of half an orange
6 – 8 teaspoons of icing sugar

Once again, deploy the whizzy doofer, chuck all the ingredients in together and give them a good blast. Then pour the mixture into the lined loaf tin and cook in the oven for 50 minutes. Allow to cool.

Mix the juice of half an orange with enough icing sugar to make a thin icing that you can dribble over the top of the cake much as you would a lemon drizzle cake. You will have to do this by trial and error to work out how sugary you prefer your icing to be.

Then pour yourself a cuppa (caffeine or not it's up to you) and enjoy.

On a totally unrelated note, one of my lovely friends at the WI did recently ask innocently (not) if I knew that you could buy lemon drizzle gin…. I didn't but I do now! I couldn't possibly comment as to whether that would make an acceptable accompaniment for this cake, but do let me know what you think if you try it. ☺ x

About the Author
Alice May

At 45 years old, Alice May is a working mother with four not-so-small children.

She is fortunate enough to be married to (probably) the most patient man on the planet and they live in, what used to be, a ramshackle old cottage in the country.

Her conservatory is always festooned with wet washing and her kitchen full of cake.

She is currently training for her black belt in Taekwondo.

Inspired by true-life events and fuelled by some really frantic painting sessions the story of 'the house that sat down' wouldn't leave her alone until it was written.

She hopes you enjoy it.

If you have any comments about this book please send them to: alicegmay@hotmail.com
Website: www.alicemay.weebly.com
Twitter: @AliceMay_Author
Or find Alice May's author page on Facebook.

P.S. Please note that no Barbarians were harmed during the writing of both 'Accidental Damage' and 'Restoration'.

More by Alice May

If you are interested in hearing more from Alice May, she is currently writing the third and final novel in 'The House That Sat Down' series which will be published in the autumn of 2018. Alice has another completely unrelated fictional novel planned for 2019.

In the meantime she is involved in presenting her Signature Talk 'Surviving the House That Sat Down' to a number of social clubs and groups. (Please see the website for details www.alicemay.weebly.com .)

Alice also exhibits and sells her original artwork and volunteers at a local children's art club.

As you no doubt know, 'Accidental Damage' and 'Restoration' were inspired by a true story. Alice May and her family really did live in the garden for well over a year after their home collapsed.

It proved to be a surprisingly entertaining experience.

And finally....

Read on for more information on the inspired teen / tween fiction stories written by Chaos (the ones Alice mentions in chapter 5 of Restoration).

She really did write them from her hospital bed and Alice loves them, although she will admit that there is a chance she is biased. Nevertheless they are still really rather good!

So, without further ado, Alice May is privileged to introduce:

The 'Victoria Institute' Series

by the teen novelist:

H. T. King.

Book One: Undercover Thief

Pamela Torres has been breaking the law since she was nine years old. Left alone in London, needing to steal to survive, Pamela has managed to make a life for herself.

Then, one day, Pamela's parents turn up again and turn her whole world upside down. They enrol her in a school, but this school is unlike any school that Pamela has ever heard of before. The Victoria Institute isn't just any school. It's a school for spies!

Book Two: Thief Underground

Being a thief and a spy was never going to be easy, nevertheless Pam thinks she's been juggling her two lives and two families fairly well.

Until now!

When Jerry and Leah are kidnapped, Pam abandons her friends, her parents and the Victoria Institute to rescue them, falling back into her old life and old friends in the Underground. Now Pam has to complete a job set by a man who refuses to identify himself, before time runs out. If that wasn't hard enough, she has to do it whilst trying to out run her parents with Jerry and Leah's lives hanging in the balance.

Printed in Great Britain
by Amazon